COMPROMISE

HOLLY HANDS

WESTBOW
PRESS
A DIVISION OF THOMAS NELSON

WestBow Press books may be ordered through booksellers or by contacting:

WestBow Press
A Division of Thomas Nelson
1663 Liberty Drive
Bloomington, IN 47403
www.westbowpress.com
1-(866) 928-1240

ISBN: 978-1-4497-1278-5 (sc)
ISBN: 978-1-4497-1279-2 (e)

Library of Congress Control Number: 2011922283

Printed in the United States of America

WestBow Press rev. date: 5/10/2011

This book would not be a success without the following individuals:

Dad and Mom,

You're unconditional support is beyond anything that can ever be repaid. God truly knew what he was doing when he decided to bless me with you as parents. And I am beyond thankful everyday. Your faith has carried our family through all of the hardships we have endured, and will always continue to do. Trust always in Him, he has proven his love and faithfulness time and time again.

Grandma V. Schock

Thank you Grandma for your encouragement as I journeyed through this process. You unknowingly, have been my toughest critic, and helped me to realize that this dream of mine was possible. If Violet, who had read many books, could love this story, so would the rest of the world. I am honored to have named one of my most important characters after you combined with Grandma Hands.

Jane Carlson

Thank you Jane, for your support and encouragement. I am thankful for the recent years of friendship we have established together. You have helped to inspire a dream, and see the fulfillment of it, and for that I will always be appreciative. You hold a very dear place amongst the Hands family, and forever will.

Sherry and Alice Wilson

As my second mom and adopted sister and best friend, I am always unconditionally thankful for our friendship. Ally I am so glad that you have been there through every moment, bad and good. Thank you for the years of gut wrenching laughter, support, and a listening ear. There is no one else in the world I would have for my best friend. Sherry, I am honored to adopt you as my second mother, and look forward to the many memories that await us. You are both beautiful people, and I admire you for it.

Shanna Shanahan

I am forever grateful for your friendship throughout these recent years. For your support and heart to heart advice that helped me to reestablish confidence. Your family has brought many smiles and laughter to my life. You alone have helped me to understand and appreciate the role of a woman as a wife and mother. Your family is forever blessed to have you, and someday your children will acknowledge the same.

Pam

Thank you for your willingness to be bluntly honest in all circumstances. As a teacher and now personal friend, you have helped me to see faith in uncertainty, past doubt to hope and confidence. Forever I will always remember your rugged advice to pull up my big girl panties and deal with it! A few words of advice that will forever be a motivator while placing a reassuring smile upon my face. May you experience many blessings in your new journey in life, you are most deserving of them!

Andrea Darling and Sheela Cox

Thank you for your support and excitement for me as I journey through this process. You have both been a great encouragement. You're opinions and insight helped to structure this story for its better. I miss you greatly, and look forward to our next visits, whenever God may allow it.

Elisa Lucke

Your friendship is held dear to me. I forever will admire your deep faith with God, your love for him, and your desire to always carry out his will for your life. I will never have such a spiritual example again in my life such as you. May you and Matthew have many blessed years ahead of you as you begin your life together.

Mrs. P. Roth

There are not enough words to describe my deep appreciation and thankfulness for your last minute editing. Thank you for your willingness and your efforts. A manuscript of this size demanded much time and attention. You will always be remembered as a major influence in the process of this publishing.

Members of the New Leipzig Baptist Church

Thank you for your prayers, your support, interest and concern throughout this entire process. It will always be forever appreciated. This story could never have been a success, no matter how great, or small, without your earnest prayers.

ONE

Hayden Alterson sighed as he stared at the ceiling above him, contemplating the numerous ways to salvage what he could of sleep before his alarm was set to go off in a few short hours. For the past few weeks, sleep had seemed to evade him. As he laid there, he marveled at just how wonderful sleep used to be. Sleep agents had helped the first few times, but when they too had seemed to lose their effect, he had stopped taking them.

Tired of being awake and restless, afraid he would wake Carly, he threw back the covers and got out of bed. Wearily, he scratched his stomach as he walked out of their room. He hadn't even made it halfway down the hallway before their golden retriever Sal met him. Pressing his nose against Hayden's palm, Sal sat down and looked at him, whining just loudly enough to be heard.

"Shhh." Hayden covered the dogs mouth with the palm of his hand, "you'll wake her." Sal's ears perked up at the sound of Hayden's voice, his eyes full of emergency combined with everlasting patience. "Do you have to go out?" The pink tongue emerged to lick the sides of Sal's mouth; and again, Sal whined, stretching out his front legs so they touched Hayden's feet.

"Come on." Hayden moved further down the hallway, leading the way to the garage through the living room, then kitchen. Attempting to be as quiet as possible, he opened the side garage door, watching Sal burst past him with a force of anxious energy.

As he leaned against the doorframe, waiting for Sal to finish, he took in a deep breath, feeling the dampness of an early spring morning before sunrise.

Of all the seasons, he loved spring. Spring meant the shift of change to summer sun and warmth, the promise of new, fresh beginnings, but more importantly, the coming close to an NHL hockey season. It wasn't that he disliked playing hockey, he loved it, had loved it since childhood when his father had placed a stick in his hands. But the pace as an NHL player began to take its toll. Every year he looked forward to spring, looked forward to Being able to sit back and relax a bit, to breathe, and marvel at how wonderful it felt to simply sit back, eat what he wanted for a short time, mindless of the dietary guidelines that his athletic body required. To simply sit and enjoy the company of family, not having to board a plane every few days, hopping from city to city.

But this spring was different. This spring, they actually stood a chance at being in a playoff position. From childhood he had watched others before him lift the Stanley Cup, holding the glinting honor for all to see. In the world of NHL, it truly meant you were the best. That you had been able to over come all of the challenges you were faced with. That you had had the heart combined with ambition and determination to achieve a win. Had somehow managed to do everything right despite all of the imperfections. That the lengthy season filled with injuries, penalties and mistakes hadn't been for nothing.

Since childhood he had dreamed of playing in the NHL, dreamed of playing alongside the men he had grown up watching on television. Dreamed of being the captain who hoisted the Stanley Cup before the home crowd. And for the first time since being drafted, since beginning his NHL career, he was finally seeing the possibility that his dream might become a reality.

But it was a reality that hung by a fragile thread. Anxiously he sighed. He thought he had been covering his secret well, thought he had been making the right moves, keeping the right distance and attitude around Lacey while at work. But obviously, he had slipped up, hadn't managed to hide his true feelings as well as he had thought. And maybe it wasn't him; maybe it was Lacey.

A familiar frustration began to rise as he thought about his affair. To this day, he couldn't understand what had brought him to this point. He had never intended to hurt Carly, had never in his entire life dreamt that he would be one of those men who cheated on their wife. But he was. It hadn't taken much, a simple forfeit of strength and self control had lead to a single-night-stand in a hotel room.

Lacey was intoxicating, hard to say no to. She had appeared at the right moment, a moment where his guard and vulnerability as a man had been clearly visible. After that first night he had told himself it would never happen again. He had honestly decided that he was going to tell Carly, but when he had finally brought himself to a point to admit everything to her, the words hadn't come. He had stood before her and brought up a completely casual point.

After that, Lacey had become a regular occurrence. He knew that the circumstances of his marriage were no excuse to begin an affair, but yet they explained it.

After the accident, Carly had pushed him away, refused to let him in. Confused and hurt himself, struggling with the grief that consumed him, he had floundered as he struggled to discern just how to help his wife. When he couldn't find a way to help her, he had dived into complete anger and frustration. Frustration not only at her but with himself. He loved his wife, more than anything in this world. He had strived to protect and care for her, financially, materially and physically. With his profession, he was able to provide her with anything that she desired. But the one thing that she absolutely wanted in this world he was unable to give her.

Carly had dreamed of being a mom since her own childhood. While they had been dating, Hayden had witnessed how she was with children, and just how much she loved them. Any chance she had she was around children. He had dreamed of marrying her, starting a family, watching her be a mother to their children.

He had never been so overjoyed and happy in his entire life the day he learned of their first pregnancy. Relieved and thankful beyond expressible words that finally they would have a child of their own. Nine months later, their son, Wyatt had been born strong and healthy. In the first new seconds of holding him, he was amazed by the amount of love for his new son that overwhelmed him.

It had been a joy to watch him grow, learning to roll, crawl and then walk. There had been nothing greater than watching his chubby cheeks wrinkle with his bright smile. His first birthday arrived and passed, the pictures taken to line the new photo albums. Then, two short years later, a few days short of his third birthday, everything had changed.

Carly had been on her way home, after Hayden's game. Wyatt had fallen asleep in his car seat. While stopping at an intersection waiting for the light to change, Carly had briefly glanced back at him, conscious of the second child she carried. She had been stopped only seconds, when the drunk driver collided with her.

Having been speeding, Carly was hit with enough force to roll the car, rolling until it finally collided with another vehicle, where it rested.

Hayden received the call while walking through the front door of his home. There still were not words to describe his horror as he walked into the hospital, where he learned that Carly had needed surgery after her abrupt miscarriage due to trauma. Aside from a few broken ribs, and a concussion, she would be fine.

It had been the next news that shattered his life forever. Wyatt had died instantly. He hadn't been able to grasp the full realization of the fact, but the agony brought the tears. He had sat by Carly, mourning the loss of their unborn child, and the loss of Wyatt.

Everything had changed that day. What had once been a healthy, thriving relationship, soon shriveled. The Carly that had once talked to him about anything and everything suddenly had nothing to say to him. After returning home from the hospital, Carly had turned and looked at him to say simply, "It happened, we move on." And walked away from him.

Even though she had attempted to cover up her pain, he had known better. She had busied herself with work again, focusing on any small detail that would keep her time occupied. Not once did she stop or take a break in her busy schedule, unless it was for sleep or a bathroom break. But even at night, as he had wrapped his arms around her, holding her close, he had heard her quieted sobs when she had thought him to be asleep.

He had never felt so frustrated and at a loss in his entire life. Everything up until that point had been easy, school, relationships of any kind, his career, and Carly. He had always known the answer to every problem, could fix any problem with little effort or thought. But this problem, hadn't been one that he could easily fix; the solution evaded him.

Eventually, Carly had simply stopped talking to him. Eventually, he had done the same. He focused on his career, while she did the same, their unspoken frustrations and hurt suppressed until it had taken shape in a completely different form. How he had ever found the capability to be as harsh as he had been still was incomprehensible to him. The things he had said, the things he had done.

He hadn't simply managed to hurt Carly with words, but he had succeeded in hurting her emotionally. His affair had started as a compromise to the morals and values he had believed in, a mistake that could never take back. The mistake that held major consequence if ever exposed.

Consequences that stood to ruin everything he had managed to build. And yet, that fear in itself was seemingly ineffective to helping him stop. Lacey provided an escape, she was fun, easy to talk to, she understood him. But she wasn't Carly, and she wasn't his wife..

He was bored with her, tired of the lies and the constant checking and covering up he found himself doing. There had to be a way out, a way to end everything without it resulting in a complete disaster, without exposing the affair.

The answer however to ending his affair, evaded him, and again, the horrible little thought made its way to the surface. He wasn't even entirely sure he wanted to end things with Lacey.

No one had found out yet; no one knew; so there couldn't be much harm in continuing on with things as they were. As he walked back up to his room, finally sure that he would be able to sleep, he smiled as he sighed and a small sense of relief began to fill him.

His secret, was perfectly safe, no one was going to find out. There was absolutely no need to ruin a completely perfect thing.

Two

Carly Alterson had just finished emptying the dishwasher when the phone began to ring. Curiously, she reached across the counter, "Hello?" she answered, wondering who was taking the time to call her.

"Hello Carly, it's Dr. Monroe."

She swept a loose strand of hair back behind her ear as she leaned against the counter, a smile easing its way across her face, "Hello Dr. Monroe, how are you?" She had had a doctor's appointment three days ago, but Dr. Monroe had had to cut the appointment short, having spent the morning at the hospital, which meant his regular appointments had been delayed. He had ordered some tests, which had included a blood test, and was now finally calling to let her know the results.

"I'm good, but more importantly, how are you?" he asked carefully.

Carly wasn't sure what she detected in his voice, but it was enough to make her slightly nervous, "Feeling the same. I'm still nauseous and haven't been able to eat much. The headaches are still coming and going, and I'm feeling tired, more exhausted, so nothing has really changed." She had scheduled the appointment with her physician because of her inability to recover from the flu that had plagued her a month and a half ago. When there was a short period of silence, she asked, "Is there anything I should be concerned about Dr. Monroe?"

"No, Carly, there isn't anything seriously wrong. The tests that I ordered came back normal, in fact you are perfectly healthy." He paused, allowing her to absorb the information.

Confusion began to cloud her thoughts. If she was perfectly healthy then why did she feel so exhausted? Something had to be wrong. "I'm sorry Dr. Monroe, I don't understand. I shouldn't feel this way if I'm perfectly healthy."

"Well, you would feel that way Carly, if you were pregnant." He paused again.

She felt her heart drop, "If I were pregnant?"

"Yes, Carly, congratulations! You are pregnant."

The words hit her like a slap to the face. They stung and left her in utter confusion, pregnant? "Are you sure?" Carly heard herself ask.

"Yes, I am sure. It explains why you are feeling nauseous, the headaches, the exhaustion. You aren't that far into the pregnancy, but your body is beginning to adjust to this new presence in your body. It was perfectly reasonable for you to attribute your symptoms to the flu you had a month and a half ago although it's not medically known for a flu to last a month and a half."

She caught the hinting and joking tone behind his comment, but failed to smile, "I can't be pregnant." She responded.

"And why not?" he asked her.

"Because," she threw her free hand into the air, pressing it against her forehead, "I medically cannot have a child."

There was a sigh, "Well, Carly, despite what the specialists said and believed after your first pregnancy and miscarriage, you are medically capable of conceiving."

She felt the air leave her lungs as she slid down the cupboards to sit on the floor, "I simply can't be pregnant." She forced herself to think, to focus, but the only word that kept pounding through her thoughts was *pregnant*. "Dr. Monroe, even you said I would never have children, I simply can't be pregnant."

"Carly the news we delivered a year and a half ago was absolute. We thought for sure after the surgery your chances of getting pregnant were next to impossible. But, here you are, a year and a half later, pregnant."

"I'm not supposed to be though." The words escaped her mouth. They hadn't planned on having children. They had accepted it, moved on, in their own ways. There was no way their marriage was stable enough to endure bringing a child into.

A sigh filled with annoyance huffed through, "Carly, as your doctor, I am telling you that you are pregnant. At some point you are going to have to believe that."

I wasn't supposed to get pregnant though. The thought pounded through her head along with the single word. "You said if I ever did it would be high risk."

"Well, yes, I did." She heard him tapping his fingers against his desk, "Carly, it has been a year and a half. Some people recover well; we'll take this slow, see how you do along the way. But at this point Carly, I see nothing to be concerned about. Listen Carly, I have a few other phone calls to make, but my congratulations to you and Hayden. You are going to make wonderful parents, I'll have one of the receptionists call you later to schedule your first appointment."

"First appointment?"

"Pre-natal care Carly." He said calmly.

"Right." Was all she could manage to say, her head was swirling in every possible direction; it simply wasn't true. It was a dream. She would wake up in a few seconds. But when she closed her eyes and opened them again, she was still in her kitchen on the phone with a doctor who was telling her that she was pregnant.

"Carly? Are you still there?"

"Yes, I'm still here…um, Dr. Monroe?"

"Yes, Carly?"

"Please don't tell anyone." An awkward silence fell between them at the request.

"That is what our confidentiality contract is in place for Carly. I couldn't tell anyone if I wanted to." He chuckled lightly, "Well, Carly, again I have a few other calls to make, so I need to be going." he said warmly.

"Dr. Monroe." She insisted again, "You're sure?"

He laughed this time, "Yes, Carly, I am sure."

"Good bye Dr. Monroe." She hung up, hearing him say goodbye. She stared ahead at the oak cupboard door, pregnant? She was pregnant. She shook her head, no, she simply wasn't. She couldn't be having a baby, not now. Not with things as they were. Hastily she stood up, how could she possibly believe Dr. Monroe? There simply had to be a mistake, they had accidentally switched her results with someone else's.

After a mad search for her car keys, she climbed behind the wheel and placed the key in the ignition. As she backed out of their driveway to head out of their suburb into major traffic, she signaled to merge, then set cruise as she traveled down the expressway. It simply wasn't possible. She had been so careful. Had done everything right. Hayden didn't want children, at least not now. She didn't want children, although admittedly, more and more lately she had been considering it. But that didn't mean she actually *wanted* children.

And besides, Hayden was gone on the road most of the time, being only four weeks away from playoffs. He was rarely home, if he was he was at the arena for practice then he was spread throughout Winnipeg for interviews with this magazine and that TV show. Sometimes he was even at commercial shoots. They were busy, she had her career, Hayden had his. There simply wasn't any time for a baby.

The thoughts rushed through her head like the traffic she found herself driving with. She and Hayden weren't even getting along. They were fighting constantly. She avoided going home, picking up later shifts just so she could avoid him. She talked to him when she had to. Painted the smile across her face at receptions, banquets and social events hosted by the NHL or the NHL wives. In public they were very much the happily married couple, madly in love. But behind closed doors, it was the furthest thing from their very public image.

She signaled to pull into the parking lot of a pharmacy, where she hoped desperately that no one would notice or recognize her. As she walked in she headed straight for the pregnancy tests. Anxiously, she grabbed one, convincing herself that she couldn't rely on what Dr. Monroe had told her, even though she believed his word as if it were the Bible.

Impatiently she waited inline at the check out, ignoring the look from the cashier as she swiped the kit. "Have a good day." She heard the young woman say, but she didn't bother to reply to the courteous greeting.

Anxiously she climbed into her car and again, merged with traffic. How would she tell Hayden? What was there to tell him? She wasn't even sure if she was pregnant, although, she had to be after all. Dr. Monroe wouldn't make up something like that. Besides, all the facts matched and added up, regardless of the fact that she had taken the birth control faithfully. She hadn't paid much attention when she had skipped, and it didn't help matters that Hayden had actually cared enough to make love to her nearly a month ago.

How could she not have considered the fact that she might be pregnant? She felt suddenly embarrassed. Every woman who was sexually active should know whether or not to even consider pregnancy a possibility. But she honestly hadn't. She had been busy, preoccupied with other things. Pregnancy or getting pregnant had never been on her priority list as compared to some women her age.

Angrily, she turned on the radio, hoping some music would help to distract her suddenly tumultuous thoughts. Her life had been somewhat simple as of thirty minutes ago. Now, everything was completely upside down.

Twenty minutes later as she pulled back into her suburb then into her own driveway. She made sure that Hayden hadn't come home while she had been gone then parked the car in the garage. Anxiously, she reached for the pharmacy bag then ran upstairs, ignoring their golden retriever who met her at the door.

In the safety of her own bathroom, she pulled the kit from the bag, reading the instructions. According to the instructions it would be better to wait until morning, but she didn't have that kind of time or patience. She needed to know now. If she was pregnant, she was pregnant. The time of day that of which she took the test wouldn't influence the results. A pregnant woman was a pregnant woman despite the time.

After completing the test she waited the stated amount of time, then picked up the stick. She felt the air leave her lungs as she read the positive results that seemed to scream at her. She sat down on the toilet, throwing the stick back into the box, stashing it cleverly in the trashcan so that Hayden wouldn't see it.

What would she do now? She was pregnant. Pregnant. She was about to have a child, Hayden's child. She simply wasn't ready to be a mother. It wasn't fair to bring a child into a situation like theirs. What good parents could they ever possibly hope to be if they couldn't talk to each other without screaming? It took two parents to raise a child, she couldn't do something like that on her own. She needed Hayden to be there, to be with her as she brought this child into the world and raised it.

There were so many questions, so many thoughts, many things to suddenly worry about. And so little time to answer them all. The only thing that seemed evident was that she had to tell Hayden. He deserved to know, but how and when to tell him evaded her. Sighing, she convinced herself that it could wait. She hadn't even brought herself to believing that she was indeed pregnant, even after two tests. She felt the tears beginning to stream down her cheeks.

"I'm pregnant." She whispered the words out loud, shuddering at just how realistic they suddenly made everything seem. She simply couldn't be pregnant. And yet she was, and for the first time since she had heard the news that had seemed to shake her world, she allowed the bitter news to sink in, and began to slowly embrace it.

She was pregnant. And she hadn't the slightest idea what to do.

Three

Mandy Alterson placed a cup of steaming fresh brew roasted coffee in front of her husband, "Good morning." She leaned forward to place a kiss on his cheek.

"Good morning." He smiled at her as he picked up the cup, "You just continue to astound me." He took a sip of the coffee, savoring it's taste.

"Why? Because I bring you coffee?" she laughed as she took a bite of her raisin bagel as she carefully climbed back into bed beside him.

"Yes." His eyes danced with their own laughter as he turned back to his newspaper. "You saved this old man a trip down the stairs."

"You are the furthest thing from old." She raised an eyebrow sarcastically, "What hurts this morning?"

"Well, everything." He didn't look away from his paper, "Let's just say I was the primary target of hits last night, by men who are twice my size."

"You are a huge man yourself. I doubt they were twice your size." She sighed as she stared ahead at the wall "Did you win last night?" She had been asleep when he had gotten home. She had intended to wait up for him, but having to work the extra shift last night had left her beyond exhausted.

"No." he held the morning's paper for her to see, "And I'm reminded of it."

She skimmed her way through the sports report then looked back at him, "That bad of a game?"

"Well, it wasn't so much about it being bad really. It was just that we couldn't pull ourselves together. We had 34 shots on net last night, but only one of those trickled past Niemi. Nick put up a huge game for us, blocked 40 shots out of 43. He had some amazing saves last night." Calvin allowed his mind to wander to memories of the previous nights game. It had been a challenging game, mentally but more so physically; he had the aches and pains to remind him just how physical it had been.

"Who scored the one goal for the team?"

"Gallagher." Calvin turned to face his wife then, suddenly remembering just exactly what he had wanted to talk to her about. "I heard something yesterday afternoon."

"And what did you hear?" The topic of sudden interest wasn't all that interesting for her. Calvin was always hearing things, and she had never liked participating in the gossip circles that seemed to thrive in every town she had lived in.

"About Hayden." Calvin raised his eyebrows, knowing that much alone would catch his wife's interest.

"Hayden?" she set her bagel down, her full attention on what he was about to say next.

"There's a rumor floating around the franchise that Hayden is being a little to friendly with some of the women reporters we sometimes find ourselves being interviewed by for the intermission reports." Calvin allowed time for the words to sink in.

"Friendly as in, an affair?" Mandy stretched to connect the dots, and her voice reflected her uncertainty.

"Well, that's a bit of a stretch." Calvin laughed, "I don't think they mean in that sense. Just friendly in the sense that it's inappropriate for a married man to be showing that much attention."

Mandy took a moment to look at her husband, "And what do you think?" he knew his brother better than she did. There were always rumors circulating in the professional sports world, for any professional athlete. There couldn't be much to these new rumors. Hayden was always the topic of conversation and gossip; even her own husband was.

Calvin took a long sip of his coffee, "I don't know what to think any more Mandy."

"What do you mean?" Mandy was slightly shocked by the statement. Her own husband wasn't sure what to think? He knew as well as she did that most things heard in the NHL circles were never true. Hayden wasn't that type of man. He simply wasn't.

"He's my brother, I know him better than anyone in this world, with the exception of our parents. He's just not himself lately, that's all." Calvin met his wife's gaze, and read the expression that screamed at him, "That's not to say that I think that the rumors are true. I know as well as you do that you can't believe anything you hear these days, but Mandy, I'm just not sure any more."

His brother had changed, that much was true, but she hadn't thought he had changed for the worse. "Have you talked to him lately?"

"No, we see each other in practice, before the game, on the ice during the game, and in the locker room afterwards. He's always being interviewed, and doing commercials and meeting for this appointment or that. He's a busy man."

The comment stuck out at her for some reason, and the longer she thought about it, it began to come back to her, Carly had said something yesterday when she had picked up the kids, "Carly said something the other day that I thought was strange. She made the comment in passing, so I'm not sure it was completely serious or ill intended, but she just seemed frustrated. She said that I was lucky to be able to count on the fact that you were coming home at some point. That Hayden was never home any more. Always doing this and that for everyone else."

Calvin hadn't talked to Carly in awhile, Mandy saw her most of the time simply because she had to pick up the kids or drop them off, "Sounds like a jealous comment if you ask me."

"Mhmm." Mandy nodded as she picked up her bagel again, finishing off the last few bites. "You think everything is okay with those two?" she asked after a few minutes had passed.

"Why wouldn't they be?" Calvin didn't look away from his paper.

"Just wondering, it's always a possibility you know. Maybe I should drop by this afternoon and talk to her. Actually talk to her, not just in passing like all the other times."

"How is Carly?" Calvin thought to ask then. Because he hadn't talked to her or Hayden in awhile, he didn't even know how either of them were doing.

"Well, when I picked up the kids last night, Carly seemed distracted. She was her typical self, it just seemed like her mind was in another place. The kids were happy and had nothing bad to say, so I decided it was nothing to worry about." Mandy answered carefully.

Calvin nodded, "She was probably tired."

"She's still sick. She mentioned that she went to the doctor and they gave her some medication that she's hoping will make a difference." Mandy took a moment then to glance at the clock, "I should go get the kids up for school."

"It's that time of day already?" Calvin stared at the clock now, wondering where the time had gone.

"It is." Mandy leaned over to kiss him, savoring the moment of quiet and instant peace she felt. "I love you." She whispered.

"And I love you." He whispered back, kissing her again.

She pulled away from him, smiling as she climbed down from the bed, "Fruit loops and backpacks and fighting over who gets to wear what for the day. The things I live for!" she commented in passing as she walked out of their bedroom.

Calvin allowed his smile to fade even when he heard her greet their children for the morning. Truth be told, he was worried about his brother, but he wasn't about to admit that to his wife. He wasn't even sure there was anything to be worried about. "What is it God?" he whispered as he folded his newspaper, "Why am I so worried?" Silence answered.

As he too climbed out of bed, dressing in his running clothes in preparation for his morning run, his thoughts returned again to his brother. Slightly frustrated that he couldn't think about anything else, he sat down on the edge of his bed. His mother had told him when he was a child that if he couldn't stop thinking about someone, he should probably be praying for them. He hadn't fully adopted the idea until he had grown into adulthood.

"God, for some reason or another, my brother is in my thoughts constantly. I try to think of other things, but he just keeps coming back. I don't know what Lord, but something doesn't seem right. I worry about him God. But I know that He is in Your hands alone. God whatever he is facing whatever is happening in his life right now, I ask that you work in the situation, that you would let Him know you are there, and how much you love him. Amen."

Four

Lacey Peterson hummed the chorus of her favorite song as she slipped into the red-laced lingerie she had picked up yesterday afternoon at a small boutique that she had made a habit of frequenting. She smiled as she felt the delicate material cling to her body, admiring the curves she had achieved through three years of dedicated workouts. Being in the media and public eye everyday demanded your best appearance, a healthy, sexy appearance that she prided herself on.

Satisfied that everything was finally in place, she turned to study herself in her full-length mirror. Flashing the flirtatious smile she had practiced all her life, she flipped her mid-length auburn hair behind her right shoulder and made a point of sticking out her hips. The small action allowed her curves to show in all the right ways. Finally, she stood straight, placing her hands on her hips, admiring just how good the lingerie looked against her toned, tanned body. It was definitely worth keeping, and wearing. She had known it would, but she never knew for sure until she had tried it on at home.

Delicately, she began stripping the pieces off of her body, reaching for the sweat pants and t-shirt she had resorted to wearing for the day. Every day of the week required her to be dressed perfectly without a flaw, looking fashionable yet businesslike at the same time. Her days off were her freedom. As much as she loved her work, loved being the center of attention in front of a camera beside some of the professional sports athletes, she craved for the days when she could walk around her apartment without any makeup, wear loose clothing, and be normal in every sense that normal was.

But today was anything but a normal day off. She had plans, big plans that had her excited to her very core. As she walked into her bathroom to begin applying the makeup routine that accentuated her even, delicate features, she allowed her mind to wander to the thoughts of what lay ahead for that evening.

She was about to spend the night with NHL's super star Hayden Alterson again, and she could barely wait. There was no other feeling like having his athletic arms wrapped around her, pulling her close, holding her all through the night. And there was no way to possibly describe just how amazing he was in bed. She allowed a smile to sweep across her face at just that thought alone. He was the complete package, the man every woman involved in the sports world wanted. Good looking, beyond average, with his deep, piercing blue eyes, the hazel hair that seemed to style itself. A character that was sensible, demanded respect, fair and kind, yet determined, and flawlessly reputable.

Reputable of course, with a small exception.

No one knew of the affair. For three months they had kept the dirty secret from the prying eyes and desperate ears of the media. Because he was Hayden Alterson and she Lacey Peterson, the story that could come from finding out their secret would be beyond scandalous. The media would have a story to write about for months. She no doubt would be fired for being sexually involved with a professional athlete. It stated in her contract that she was to remain professional at all times. She thought it was horribly unfair that the rule seemed to stretch into her personal life. That was one disadvantage to her career. Being in the spotlight meant that she had no personal life. Career and personal were intertwined. Her career affected the personal and vice versa. She had to be careful at all times.

But careful had flown out the window the minute she had found out that she was being transferred to cover the NHL. It was too good to be true. She had accomplished her dream. Her hard work had finally paid off. But only one thing came to mind, Hayden Alterson. She had known him before he had become the NHL Super Star that he was. She was best-friends with his wife Carly, having developed their friendship throughout their college careers together.

But when Carly had met Hayden their friendship had changed in a way that she to this day didn't understand. Admittedly, a part of her had always been jealous. She had tried to understand how someone like Carly could have managed to land a relationship with the most popular man at school, not to mention the hottest athlete with the most talent. Everyone then had known he was destined for the NHL.

But the closer Hayden and Carly had become, the closer Carly had become with her as well, and she had gotten to know Hayden as well. She had always liked him, dreamed of being with him herself. But she had never dreamt of taking away the one thing Carly loved most.

When she found out about their engagement, she had congratulated them both, but transferred to a school in the states to forget about Hayden and focus on being a true best friend. She had attended the wedding and stood as the maid of honor for Carly.

But then her career had allowed her to return home to Winnipeg. And quickly, she had become involved once again in Carly's life, attempting to regain time they had lost after she had transferred. There was only one problem. Hayden.

It had happened by accident, really. She had happened to attend a party one evening and ran into Hayden, standing outside, alone. She hadn't known that Carly and Hayden had planned to attend. She had planned to walk away before he noticed her, but he had. After exchanging a simple greeting she stuck around for the sake of politeness. Knowing full well that her feelings for Hayden were bound to surface and take over if she didn't distance herself.

But the conversation had taken an interesting turn. Hayden began to confess that he wasn't happy with his marriage. It had been then that she had realized he was slightly drunk, but that hadn't mattered to her. She had realized the opportunity then but had disregarded it, knowing that she couldn't hurt Carly in that way.

But hurting Carly had proven to be easier than she had ever imagined. Hayden had run into her again and again, and finally one night, her feelings got the best of her, and she had awaken the next morning beside Hayden in a cheap hotel room. They were both hung over, but the evident apparentness of what had happened was obvious.

The guilt that had overwhelmed her had been suffocating. Hayden had sat on the edge of the bed, panicking. Finally, they had agreed that they would carry on with their lives, saying nothing, forgetting about it.

But it had happened again, and then again, and finally had escalated into a full blown affair. Now, Carly was the furthest thing from her mind. All she wanted was Hayden. And she didn't care anymore if that meant sleeping with her best friend's husband. She loved the way he made her feel, admiring the safety and security his arms provided. There was nothing or anyone else to compare it to. She had been with plenty of men, but Hayden was different.

She knew she should feel guilty, knew she should feel some sense of remorse for her actions, the choices she had made; but she didn't. She had no regrets, nothing to take back, nothing to be sorry for. It was time that she had started looking out for herself and meeting her needs rather than her best friend's.

As she applied a thick coating of lip gloss, she pressed her lips together firmly to even out the coating. Soon, Hayden would leave, and come to be with her, forever. But when that would be, she didn't know, and she was growing impatient. It had to be soon though, she couldn't take much more of this running around secretly, paranoid about who might be around the corner to snap their picture.

But for now, in this moment, it would have to do. It was the only way she had Hayden, and for now, she would continue to put up with it all because she loved him. And if this was what it took for him to be in her life, she was willing to continue doing it, no matter the cost.

FIVE

Hayden tapped an uneven rhythm across the bench while he waited for his skates to be sharpened. He was fully dressed, his stick was taped, his laces were sitting beside him, it was just a matter of putting on his skates, and a few moments later they would be skating out onto the rink he had loved since childhood. He had been more than lucky and fortunate to be given the privilege to play professional hockey in his hometown arena. It was simply unheard of for professional hockey players to receive the opportunity of playing for their own personal, favorite team. How he had received the privilege, he wasn't sure.

As a child he had grown up watching the Winnipeg Jets nestled comfortably in his own home. His dad had been a passionate fan, and needless to say, that passion had carried over to his son. His dad had even taken him to a few games.

"Hades, you ready?" Coach Ambers looked at him with all seriousness.

"Yeah, coach." Hayden nodded his head in affirmation as he reached for his stick. He had to stay focused, lately it seemed every little thing was distracting him.

"You okay?" Nick Venther raised an eyebrow at him as he leaned down to tie his own skates.

"Yeah, I'm fine." Hayden sighed as he rested against his locker.

"You sure?" Nick pushed a little more.

"Fine, Nick." Hayden forced a smile, "Just got a lot on my mind. Nothing to be worried about though."

Nick slid a little closer to Hayden, dropping his voice to almost a whisper, "Hades, there's rumors floating around that you and that reporter from Versus are getting a little too friendly."

Hayden felt his heart skip a beat as instant panic overwhelmed him. "Where'd you hear that Nick?"

Nick shrugged, "Around. Some of the guys were talking about it earlier this morning."

"Which guys?" Hayden narrowed his eyes.

"You know, Alex and Drake."

"Has Carly heard of this yet?" Hayden asked the question before thinking about what such a question might imply for anyone listening.

A confused look crossed Nick's face, "No, not that I know of. Why?"

"No reason. Just don't want her getting upset about something that isn't true, that's all." Hayden sighed as he prided himself on the classy save. He desperately tried to think of something to switch the conversation to, "You ready to be up against Hattering tonight?"

A smile flashed across Nicks face, "More than ready. He hasn't had a real challenge up till now."

Hayden felt an easy laugh escape as he looked at Nick, the twig of a goalie that he was. Barely passing 6' 1" he stood lean like a pole. His light build however was attributed with the physical build required, but the equipment he wore added mostly to it. Compared to the other goalies in the NHL, he was what some would call tiny. His size had even earned him a nickname shortly after he had been drafted, but it had soon been replaced when it became evident that there was more to this goalie than his size. Nick's name was starting to surface more and more as his game improved. Two games in a row he had proved them with a shut out, but tonight would be a different story.

Montreal was first in their division this year, and with their broad, talented forwards, they were enough to send just a small shiver of fear through their opponents. Hattering was averaging the most ice time with the most goals scored for his team.

"Hades!" he stood at the sound of his name to cross the dressing room to grab his skates, "Thanks Tom!" he smiled at the seasoned skate sharpener who was rumored to have been with the Jets since their beginning.

"Just make sure you win tonight." He walked away from Hayden, offering the warning that Hayden had had to listen to since he had started playing for the team.

As he sat down in front of his locker to begin lacing his skates, he looked back at Nick, "You take the interview tonight."

"What?" Nick looked at him, again confusion displayed across his face.

Hayden sighed, "With Lacey Peterson. You take the interview. They'll want to talk to me, but I don't want to be bothered with an interview tonight."

"So you want me to take it? Hades, no one wants to talk to me."

"So talk to someone else. Get Alex to take the interview then." Hayden focused on tieing his skates, hoping that Nick would simply accept that that was the end to the conversation. If some of the men were gathering the opinion that he was becoming to friendly with Lacey Peterson, he needed to avoid the interview tonight. As distracted as he was tonight as well, he couldn't risk somehow blowing the lie he had struggled to build.

"Let's go boys!" Ambers yelled from outside the dressing room. "Game's on."

Hayden rushed to finish tieing his skates. He would have a few minutes during warm up to feel them out anyway. Grabbing his stick he fell into the sea of white, blue and red jerseys.

He exhaled sharply as he walked down the tunnel. When he saw Nick coming up beside him, he smiled, "Make sure to keep your eyes open tonight."

"I'll be sure to keep them closed just for you, you need a loss to deflate that cloud of ego your currently sitting on." Nick's smile faded as they skated out onto the ice.

Hayden had never really adjusted to the roar that the fans created whenever they skated out before the game began. It was deafening, and horribly distracting. But as a professional player, you found ways to block out the noise. As he skated his lap around the ice, handling and passing the puck as he went, his thoughts wandered back to Nick's earlier comment.

Was it that noticeable? Had his carefully guarded actions fallen short of camouflaging the lie he had so carefully constructed? The guard he had determinedly built and protected? He had been avoiding interviews with her the past few games, afraid that his true emotions would come through. The woman was intoxicating; there wasn't much he could do any more to resist her. So he had resorted to avoiding her.

The last thing he needed was for the whole thing to be exposed to the media, splashed across every sports news reports, harboring the covers of every tabloid in any grocery store. He was already the center of the spotlight, Super Star Hayden Alterson. He had earned that spotlight because of his unique talent and the reputable respect he had earned throughout the years playing in the NHL. Having this exposed would ruin and devastate everything he had managed to build.

He couldn't let it be exposed. As he skated back to the bench he shot a look at Drake and Alex. What could they have possibly seen or heard that would draw them to such a conclusion, especially a conclusion that wasn't that far from the truth.

Taking a moment, he glanced up to where the chairman and the members of the franchise usually sat. Carly wasn't even here tonight. And she had said that she would be. He felt the old frustration beginning to rise again and had to take a deep breath to maintain some sense of focus. After all, that was why the affair had started to begin with wasn't it? She had grown distant, had shown no interest in anything he did, spending all of her time focused on what she was doing and what she needed to do.

Granted he was gone a majority of the time, but when he was home, it was as if she didn't care at all, she barely even noticed half the time. When he was home they fought over stupid little things that weren't even worth fighting over. Lately, the only thing that kept them from fighting was his niece and nephew.

Mandy had been taking up extra shifts at the hospital where she worked. That meant that Anders and Hannah ended up at his house until Calvin was finished for the day.

"Alterson!" he looked up from his seat on the bench to see Coach yelling at him. "Get on the ice!" A glance at the scoreboard told him everything he needed to know. The game was about to start, and he was supposed to be at center ice for a face off.

He was about to skate off, when Coach yelled at him again, "Get your head in the game Alterson! Think only about hockey and what you need to do tonight to help this team accomplish a win!" He knew better than to say anything back, but Coach was right. He needed to focus, but that was proving more and more difficult with each passing day. Something was going to have to change, if it didn't, he risked losing everything.

But what that change was, he hadn't the slightest idea.

Six

Mandy knew better than to interfere with another married couple's problems. After she had married Clavin, she had become a firm believer that what took place between a married couple, whether it be a fight, or a smaller problem, or a happy event, stayed between that couple. It just didn't seem right to interfere where one really didn't belong. But she loved Carly, as her sister-in-law, and with no sisters herself, she had welcomed Carly with open arms and loved her as a sister the moment she had found out that Hayden had proposed.

Over the years, their relationships had grown and strengthened until now it seemed as if they truly were sisters, ignoring the fact that they were the wives of two men who shared a brotherly bond.

And as Carly's sister, she felt a responsibility to at least talk to Carly, find out what was currently taking place in her life, give her an opportunity to share or vent her experiences of late. Mandy's own conversation with Calvin the previous week before had left an unsettled feeling that hadn't gone away, but had steadily grown into a healthy dose of worry and concern.

Eagerly, she dialed Carly's number, and after a short conversation in which Carly had graciously allowed her to come over, Mandy hurried down the hallway to find her children. They could spend the rest of the morning over at Nancy's, her neighbor.

Together, they had reached a happy agreement that whenever the other needed to go somewhere or simply escape their children for a few hours to find relief, their children could swap houses and play with each other.

Unable to find her children inside the house, she hurried to the kitchen, where their deck lead into the backyard. Anxiously, she shielded her eyes against the sharp sun to spot her children, playing in their sandbox. "Hannah! Anders! Come here please." She called loudly enough that they would hear her. Eagerly, their small heads bobbed upwards to see their mother standing on the deck. Throwing down shovels and pails, they ran barefooted across the green grass.

"What mom!" Hannah pounded up the few steps to stand before her mother, sand clinging to her summer dress.

"Mommy!" Anders smiled as he wrapped himself around her leg, "Mommy, come play!"

She knelt down carefully, prying Anders away from her leg, "Mommy is going to visit Aunty Carly, you are going to go play with Charles and Livey, okay?"

Immediate excitement lined her daughter's face as Hannah acknowledged what her mother had just said. "Now!" she asked, her eyes wide.

"Yes, now." Mandy nodded, smiling to herself as she brought Anders closer to her, "Is that okay?" she asked him, his sudden happiness vanishing at the idea that his mom was leaving him.

He shook his head, burying his head into her shoulder, "I wanted to play with you." He sniffed quietly.

"Anders." She pulled him away holding him firmly before her, "Mommy needs you to be a big boy please. There's no need to cry." He took a moment to control himself, wiping at the sudden tears that had splashed against his rosy-red cheeks. "You don't want to go swimming with Charles?" The young neighborly boy was already showing athletic interest even at his tender age of five. Nancy had enrolled him in swimming lessons as soon as he was old enough to join, and since then, to encourage their son's developing talent, they had purchased a pool of which they had set up in their backyard. Charles spent every waking moment in that pool, of which Anders also did. Anders loved to swim, Mandy's only way of convincing him that her leaving was a good idea.

He thought carefully for a moment. "I can wear my 'pider mans pants?" he asked.

She nodded, "Yes, you can wear your spider man pants."

"Mommy!" Hannah tugged on her elbow, "What about me? Can't I go swimming to?"

"Yes, Hannah, you can go swimming too. Run inside and get your swimsuits please. I'm going to go talk to Nancy."

As they ran into the house, tearing through her kitchen, she walked through the hedges that marked the border between the two properties. Anxiously, she rang the doorbell, smiling instantly when Nancy answered. "Thank you, so much!" she admonished while she waited for her children to appear. "I can't thank you enough for taking them last minute like this."

Nancy only smiled as Charles appeared beside her, "Don't worry about it, you'd do the same. Besides, the kids were asking this morning if they could play with Hannah and Anders. It will give me a welcome break."

"Charles!" Anders came tearing through the hedges at a full run, his spider man pants flapping against his legs in the wind he was causing. "Look!" he sighed as he gasped for a breath, "I have my 'pider mans pants! We can go thimming!"

Charles gasped in excitement, "Okay!" and together the two disappeared, tearing through Nancy's entry to head to the backyard swimming pool.

After getting Hannah situated with Livey, she said her final farewells and headed back to her own house, where she searched for the keys to their Ford Escape. Finally, she was free to head over to Carly's, where she eagerly anticipated a sisterly conversation.

Carly opened the door to a smiling Mandy, whose smile only broadened as Carly embraced her in a warm hug. "It's good to see you!" she smiled calmly.

"It has been too long!" Mandy emphasized as she walked past Carly into the entry. "Sal." She patted the dog's head lightly as he sat before her, happy to be the recipient of extra attention.

"How have you been?" Carly asked as she headed into the kitchen, where she reached for some glasses to pour water into. Silently she hoped that Mandy wouldn't want anything to eat, her stomach was continually flip flopping, which was seriously deterring her from eating, even if it was just the sight or smell of food.

"I'm fine, keeping busy which is why we haven't been able to sit down and talk for so long." Mandy accepted the glass of water as she took a seat on a bar stool at the island. "Hanna and Anders miss you, they asked the other day if we could come over and visit."

Carly nodded silently to herself, having her niece and nephew over were the only times that she and Hayden managed to hold a civil conversation, in an effort to forget the thought she moved the conversation forward, "How are the kids?'

"Good, busy and tiring as always but their good. Hannah had a cold a few weeks ago, and that finally cleared up. Spring is a bad season for my kids, allergies and what not."

"They get that from their dad though." Carly smiled as she thought of Hayden rubbing his nose along with the red, puffy watery eyes that had more than once caused him to miss a practice, much to his disliking and his coach's. He and his brother were more alike than any set of brothers that she had ever personally known. They seemed to share every physical characteristic.

"Yes, they simply just couldn't gain anything from their mother." Mandy laughed lightly before taking a sip of water. "How's Hayden?"

Slightly taken aback by the question, Carly shrugged, "Fine."

"Just fine?" Mandy implored further.

Carly shifted uncomfortably, "He's busy. I don't see him as much as I'd like to, so I don't really know what's going on with him any more." She surprised herself with just how honest her response was. She had never been that honest, with anyone who asked about Hayden. Normally she just resorted to lieing.

Mandy paused before carefully asking, "Calvin's worried about him. I'm worried about you, how has everything been, honestly."

Silently she hated Mandy, for asking her to be honest. She was capable of telling a lie to anyone but Mandy. But their sister-like bond helped to establish her ability to be honest, even if the truth was brutal. She took a deep breath, "I'm thinking of leaving Hayden."

SEVEN

Mandy nearly choked on her sip of water, attempting to regain some composure, she set her glass down, "What?"

Carly nodded, "Things aren't so good Mandy. They haven't been, for awhile now. I love him, I truly do, do not think that I'm leaving him because I've fallen out of love with him, but, Mandy, our marriage is just in a horrible spot right now.

"He's gone, a lot, he's rarely home, if I do see him, if we are here, together in the same building we have nothing kind to say to one another, and that's putting it gently. We are two completely different people, who have nothing to say to one another. We fight, constantly about anything and everything. I can't relate to him. It's gotten to the point where I don't know what to do any more. I think I just need some space, away from Hayden to sort things out. Put things into perspective again."

Slightly dumbfounded from what she had heard, Mandy took a moment to absorb it all. She had known something wasn't right, that something was out of place, but nothing as serious as this. Anxiously, she took a moment to ponder what to say, "I didn't know things were this bad Carly."

A single tear slid down Carly's cheek, "I know. No one really does."

"Carly," Mandy sighed, "You should have said something earlier."

"What good would it have done?" Carly wiped away hastily the tears that were slowly spilling down her cheeks, smudging her makeup. "It's not exactly something that someone else can fix."

"Well, no." Mandy struggled to find the words to say next, "but you could have found help in other ways, I mean, you could have talked to me, we could have been praying for you. Calvin could have talked to Hayden."

Carly shook her head defiantly, "It wouldn't have done any good."

Mandy struggled to understand just how any of this was possible. They were so perfect for one another, they both loved each other more than words could express or describe, and yet, she had never imagined that their marriage would be on the brink of, well, the unsaid word in this conversation so far, divorce.

The word brought a shudder to her as she looked at Carly evenly, "Your not thinking about divorce are you?"

The tears spilled harder, "It's a thought."

The air left Mandy's lungs as she leaned back against the short backrest, "Oh Carly." She stood then, walking around the island to wrap her friend in a warm, tight embrace.

"I just don't know what to do any more Mandy." She leaned into Mandy's shoulder, "I can't talk to him. There's just so much standing between us. It's like there's this wall, that neither of us can get past. There's just so much hurt and anger and, and hatred." The words spilled easily now.

"Have you considered counseling?"

"How am I supposed to consider counseling when I can't even talk to my husband?" Carly retorted angrily. "Hayden would never go through with counseling."

Silently Mandy prayed that God would give her the words to say, some form of comfort, "Things have been bad since the accident haven't they."

Carly pulled away then, "Of course they have!" she huffed angrily, the rage and hatred spilling as she spoke, "That was my baby! My baby boy! Two years old, and his life was taken? And that baby, I wanted that baby, wanted a sibling for Wyatt, to be a mom a second time again!

"And then, then it's taken away from me. We were stripped of being parents, stripped of the only thing that I loved more than my own life!" She sniffed angrily, the hatred pouring from her now swollen eyes.

"Carly," Mandy took a step back, leaning her elbows against the counter top, "I know it was and is hard, but, there was a reason. A reason as to why God allowed that accident."

Carly's eyes narrowed. "God didn't care, if he did I would have a child turning a year old." Her chest heaved, the kept back tears once again spilling against her cheeks.

Mandy allowed a few moments of silence to settle between them, pondering what to say, or if she should say anything at all. Finally, Mandy decided it was best to be ending this conversation, to allow Carly some time and some space to think. It was obvious to her then just how bad things must be between her and Hayden. Someone this full of hate couldn't be easy to live with. That much hate and pain had to be being expressed in other ways aside from physical or verbal anger.

Biting her lip, Mandy placed a hand on Carly's shoulder, "Carly, I don't know what else to say, to tell you. But I will tell you that you have to do what you think best for you, for your marriage. If you think that is to leave Hayden for a bit, then do so. But I think you need to start talking to him, making an effort where he won't dare to." She knew her brother-in-law, too much like her own husband. If he didn't think it was worth saying anything or that his efforts wouldn't be met with positive feedback, he wouldn't say anything at all.

Carly sniffed, nodding slowly. "I'll think about it a little bit more."

Mandy glanced at the clock then, knowing she should be getting back to pick up her children. She sighed, her heart breaking in two for her friend, who was obviously hurting more than she could imagine, and for the first time in her life, she didn't have the answers. She had never felt quite this helpless or useless, she felt limited as a friend. She should be able to help especially when this situation seemed dangerously exhausted.

As she hugged Carly goodbye, she couldn't help but entertain the fleeting thought that had begun to whisper through her thoughts. What if he was having an affair? What if the rumors were true? A situation like this certainly could be the breeding ground for a compromise.

No, Hayden wouldn't dive to those extremes, wouldn't stoop to such lows. It simply wasn't like him.

EIGHT

The only reason for opening this closest was for the sole purpose of pulling a small suitcase out. Having decided that she had needed to provide herself with a distraction, she had decided to leave. To move out and put some space and distance between herself and Hayden for awhile. She needed time to think. Time to focus undistracted on herself and try to piece together a plan.

The biggest suitcase was already packed and waiting in the car, but the last few remaining items that needed packing would fit nicely in her smaller travelers case, an item that she hadn't pulled out in years. Conveniently she had placed it in the hall closet, behind the photo albums she had prioritized to look through again some day.

But as she had begun pulling the albums from the shelves, knowing that the suitcase she needed had been stored neatly behind them, she couldn't help but open the covers to reveal the pictures inside. Pictures she hadn't looked at in years. She smiled as she flipped through the photos of her and her family, the reunions, picnics, birthdays, and graduations that had passed. She had finished the first album, determined to return to packing, when she found her wedding album.

A strange emotion swept through her soul as she took a deep breath. She had thought seriously of putting that album back where it belonged, but she had continued to hold it as she tucked it securely in her arm. Eagerly, she sat down in the middle of the living room, welcoming the warmth of the sunlight as she opened the cover of the album she had set before her. The very first picture to stare back at her was of Hayden and herself. It had been a candid caption, a moment where she and Hayden had thought they had stolen a private moment to themselves. Later, after she had been showed the picture, it had become on of her favorites.

Hayden had taken a moment to lean close to whisper into her ear, the smile stretching across his face. She had glanced at the ground, laughing at what he had told her. Frozen in time, the picture reminded her of a moment that had been simple, full of pure joy and more love than she could have ever imagined.

Each page was filled with every moment of that day. From waking up, to getting ready, walking down the aisle, the vows, and the reception. Although she loved the pictures of her family, and his, it was the singles of them, that she found the most captivating.

A smile lit her face for a single instance as she remembered the man she had married. Before that, the man she had fallen in love with. The ambitious, daring, strong willed man who gave little attention to what others thought of him. Confident and strong, yet gentle and fun was what had attracted her from the very beginning.

Their meeting had been a complete accident. She had awaken from an accidental nap to find herself running late for an exam. After realizing that she had only had ten minutes to dash across campus to claim her seat, she had scrambled to gather her things, then madly rushed out of her dorm building. In the middle of December, with light snow falling, she hadn't even considered slowing down, forgetting than an icy rain and freezing temperatures had left the ground a personal skating rink two days before.

She had been halfway to her the main building, when she felt herself slip. She had fallen hard, instinctively attempting to use her arm to catch herself. She hadn't felt the crack, but the immediate pain that had followed had taken her breath away. Laying there, half in shock, she had sat up, trying to sort everything out.

"Are you okay?" a shadow had fallen beside her, and as she had glanced over to see who had witnessed her fall, her heart skipped a beat, the words stumbling pathetically over one another as the realization set in. She was talking to Hayden Alterson.

"I'm, um, no, I don't think so." The admittance had finally made its way out.

"I didn't think so; you took quite a nasty fall there. Let me help you up." He had knelt down carefully, his arm outstretched.

She had reached to grab his arm, but the instant pain that had pounded and screamed caused her to pull it back, resting it against her stomach, "I don't think I can, grab your arm."

He had knelt there for a few moments, looking at her, a strange expression clouding his steel gray eyes. Finally, he had stood again, coming around to kneel behind her, placing an arm around her waist, taking the care to try to avoid her arm. With little effort, he had helped her stand. "How badly does that arm hurt?" he had stepped around to stand in front of her, keeping his gaze leveled at the arm she was bracing.

"Bad." Was all she said. It was then that she had remembered she needed to be writing an exam. "I have to go." She bent down to pick up her bag, ignoring the instant throbbing that increased in her arm.

"Go where?" he had looked at her as if she was crazy. "Your arm is broken."

"You don't know that, I'm sure it's fine." She had turned to go, throwing her bag loosely into the crook of her arm.

"It's starting to swell you know." He raised an eyebrow at her.

"I have an exam to write, I can't afford to miss it. If I do, I have to repeat the entire semester. My whole grade is counting on that exam."

"You just fell and broke your arm, I think your first priority should be to get some medical attention." His voice had been laced with sarcasm and a hint of concern that she had found instantly annoying.

"I have to go. Thank you though." Already late for her exam, she hoped desperately that her professor would still admit her into the exam. Surely if he saw her arm he would understand.

As she had begun to walk away, he had jogged to catch up to her, "Look, you need to go see a doctor, if you don't you could make everything worse."

"I have an exam to write." She had repeated, wondering how it was so impossible for him to understand. As a student training involved in the nursing program, she knew full well that she had a broken arm, and the consequence of worsening the break if she continued to move it without seeking medical care. But her exam was more important.

"Look, let me help you." He had pleaded suddenly.

The remark had been enough to cause her to stop walking. Taking a step back, she looked at him, "Why?"

"Because you need help." He had said it so matter of factly as if she was absolutely blonde for asking such a question.

Feeling the pressure to get to her exam, and losing her patience she had finally sighed, "Alright, I'll go and write my exam, and then I'll go see a doctor."

For what had felt like forever, he hadn't said a single word, finally he said, "Fine, go and write your exam. When you're done, I'll be waiting outside to give you a ride into the city."

She had brushed the comment off, rushing ahead of him. Her professor had taken one look at her arm, a strange look crossing his face, but he had allowed her to write her exam. Finally, as she answered the last question she breathed a sigh of relief, she couldn't stand the pain any longer. Anxiously, she headed out the door to find Leah, who had agreed to take her into emergency.

But as they had both headed out of the main building, she had stopped instantly when she noticed him standing beside his car, "Took you long enough." He had called out.

Leah had turned to look at her, "That's Hayden Alterson!" the shock, excitement and confusion had all crowded her friend's expression.

"What are you doing?" she had asked then.

"Taking you in, like I told you I would."

After a short dispute and relentless persistence, she had found herself seated in the passenger seat of Hayden Alterson's car. Through the entire ride and treatment at the hospital, she couldn't bring herself to believe that the biggest athlete at their school, and not to mention the most well known man on campus had not only helped her, but had been willing to drive her into emergency and sit in the waiting room. None of it had made sense.

Shortly after her emergency experience, he had found her again, this time to invite her to one of his games, explaining that a ticket would be available if she cared to show up with a friend. Pure curiosity had driven her to attend, and as he had guaranteed, he had found her after the game. A short coffee date had resulted in an exchange of numbers, and later that week he had called.

It wasn't long until they were a steady couple. Her senior year had been enriched by his presence in her life. She had enjoyed studying with the man that had so effortlessly captivated her heart. Enjoyed getting to know him, learning about him and his life. Understanding his passions. He had been there for her through every remaining challenge up until graduation. Later that summer she had been accepted as a nurse, then, that following fall, after learning that he had been drafted to play professional hockey, he had proposed.

Her mother hadn't been completely thrilled about the news, insisting that Carly was still young, too young to even be considering marriage. But after Carly's own insistence, they had been married the following fall, after Hayden had completed his first year as an NHL player.

In that moment, five years ago, she would have never imagined their marriage and relationship together, arriving at its current state. How was it possible for two people who had loved each other as much as they had, to be at this point? Where a single word could ignite a fight that brought more tension and hurt? Where the word divorce remained unsaid, but certainly a serious thought, the point where the man she loved, her best friend, wouldn't even look at her. The man she had married and loved, was now a complete stranger, the furthest thing from the best friend she had found in him.

She had planned on spending her entire life with the man staring back at her in the photos. Had dreamt of children, love that never failed, friendship and companionship unlike anything that could be found elsewhere.

As a single tear slid down her cheek, she sighed. But no one planned for events in life that seemed to change everything. Nothing had turned out as she had imagined or dreamed. Everything had changed. Hayden wasn't the same man she had married five years ago. She wasn't the same woman. The child they were supposed to have brought into the world hadn't arrived. And somewhere along the way, life had happened. Her career had begun to thrive and develop, as had his. Soon they had been living two very separate lives.

And now here they were, five years later, their marriage a complete mess that at times she thought beyond hope or repair. She had lived her whole life thinking that every marriage was supposed to last a lifetime, even after her own parents had divorced. It had been their fault; her mother hadn't tried hard enough.

But now, she had a completely new perspective and understanding. No one planned on getting divorced. But it was a reality; a reality that was suddenly becoming horribly real, and unbearably close.

Nine

Hayden didn't glance up as he walked into the living room, his head buried in the newspaper he had grabbed from the front step as he had walked in. Having returned from practice at now noon, he knew something was out of place. Carly usually grabbed the paper before he returned home, but why she hadn't, didn't enter his mind. He had given up wondering as to why she did or didn't do things as of late.

But as he stopped beside the sofa, scanning for the remote, he noticed Carly sitting in front of the t.v, tears streaming down her face. "Carly?" he heard himself ask, silently wondering why she was crying and what could have possibly made her cry. It was unlike Carly to cry, about anything. But now, as he looked at her, her deep red hair hanging in broken curls about her face, a small emotion tugged at his heart, and a strange longing to sit down beside her and pull her into a tight embrace overwhelmed him.

"Hayden." She gasped as she hurried to wipe the tears from her cheeks. Hastily, she stood, dabbing beneath her eyes at the eyeliner that had stained her pale cheeks. "You're home."

"I'm home." The words were lifeless and awkward as he wrapped his arms around himself instead, "I'm going to go back out there." He turned to leave, but her next words stopped him.

"Hayden, I'm moving out."

He studied her carefully, an unfamiliar presence of panic and relief combining to confuse him, "You're moving out." Carefully, he measured her even gaze, mesmerized by her hazel eyes, reflecting a pain and confusion he instantly understood.

"I just, need some space, to think about things, for awhile." She wrapped her arms around her waist, "I have my things packed, and the car loaded already."

Confused, he glanced at Sal who had entered the room, if she had packed her bags and the car was loaded, why was she still here. "Why are you still here then?"

As soon as he said them, he wished he hadn't. The instant pain and anger that flashed from her now set jaw and steeled eyes let him know he had said the wrong thing.

"That's all you have to say to me." Carly took a step back, "I tell you I'm leaving, moving out for awhile, and you ask me why I'm still here, as if you don't even care."

"I didn't mean it that way." Hayden sighed as he ran a hand through his hair. No matter what he said, it came out wrong and horribly painful. He was better not to say anything. That method had seemed to work up until now.

"Well what did you mean then Hayden." She shook her head the mess of curls bouncing against her distinguished cheekbones.

While he scrambled to think of something to say, contemplating seriously a sarcastic remark, she used the sleeve of her hooded sweatshirt to wipe her nose, then turned and walked out of the room. As he realized that she was walking away from him, walking away to leave him, he jogged out behind her, watching her pull the keys from the pocket of her sweater as she opened the door.

"Carly, would you just wait a minute." Hayden dashed to place himself between her and the door, bridging himself against the frame.

"Move Hayden." She said once.

All of the things he wanted to say swirled through his head as he stared back at her even glare. There was so much that he could say, that he should have said a long time ago. But as he stood there, looking at the anger reflecting back at him, he realized that there was no point. She wanted to leave, maybe, for the time being, some space apart would be a good thing. Maybe he could gather some of his thoughts and attempt to figure out how to fix things.

With a sigh he moved out of the doorway, hanging his head as he leaned against the doorframe, watching her climb behind the wheel. As he continued to watch her start the car and pull of the drive way to disappear beyond the corner of their suburb, a strange and profound sadness overwhelmed him. But the worst was the tormenting frustration and guilt that seemed to immediately surface.

Angrily, and unsure of what to do with himself and the newfound emotions that swirled through his soul, he slammed the door shut before he walked back into the living room, where something in the middle of the carpet caught his attention. Curiously, he approached it, leaning down to pick it up. Carly must have been looking through the album before he had entered the room. It was their wedding album.

As he glanced through the photos of the day that had once meant a promise of beginning and love, he realized suddenly that the worst wasn't the sadness or the frustration, or the guilt; but the instant and sudden reality that he might have just arrived at the closest point to losing everything that had once mattered to him.

Ten

Violet Alterson sat straight up, leaning to rest against the headboard. Shaking her head as she rubbed her eyes, she acknowledged that there was no perfectly good reason as to why she had awaken from the deep sleep she had struggled to slip into hours before. As she glanced at the clock, she realized a slight tension in her chest, her breathing labored. It was then that she remembered she had been dreaming.

Anxiously she glanced over at her husband still sleeping, silently glad that she hadn't awaken him as well. Anxiously she placed a hand to her cheek, she needed to relax, needed to find a way to calm this sudden panic that overwhelmed her. Gingerly, she threw the sheets back, slipping her feet into her slippers. Quietly, she left the room, headed for the kitchen, where she poured herself a glass of water.

As she drank, the coolness refreshing her and helping her to wake up a bit more, she sat down at the kitchen table. "God." She whispered. "I'm awake, and I have no reason as to why."

Pray. Pray? She closed her eyes. At this hour of the morning, she should pray? She shook her head, attempting to clear her thoughts. There wasn't anything particularly wrong with praying at this hour of the morning. It was just something she wasn't accustomed to. A seasoned prayer warrior that she was, she had never felt that there were time limits as to when she could or couldn't pray. But just exactly what God wanted her to pray for, she didn't know. "What God? Who or what needs prayer?" she quieted her thoughts as she listened to the clicking clock behind her.

Hayden. Hayden? She opened her eyes again, a new sense of panic flooding her soul. She was supposed to pray for her son? Now? She prayed for her son every day, both of her sons, twice a day. After her husband, her sons were the most important people to her. She always prayed for them, sometimes overzealously. She smiled at the thought. Silently she wondered if God ever grew tired of hearing the constant, same prayers for her two sons.

But now, as she sat there, reaching for the worn Bible that had always sat on their kitchen table, she closed her eyes again. "God, I come before you to remember my son Hayden. And God, while I love both of my sons equally and enjoy them for the blessing you have provided in them, I am asking a special prayer for Hayden. God, my baby, my last child, I take comfort in the fact that you understand just how much I love him, how dear he is to me.

"But God, Hayden, my Hayden Lord, I don't know what to pray for him anymore." The unexpected tears and familiar fervent plea began to pour forth, "God, as you know, he doesn't walk with you. A pain God that I know pains you more than us. He has chosen to exclude us from his life as much as possible, but he is still my son, your child, who rests in your hands alone.

"Protect him God, wrap your arms around him. Whatever he is doing at this moment, even if it may be sleeping let him know how much you love him. Guide him in all his decisions. Bring healing, strength and clear thinking as well as focus so that he may be able to play his best. To use the talents that you gave him to their fullest extent. Amen." She opened her eyes, silently feeling that the prayer wasn't enough. But it was enough for her God. He knew. He understood, all that mattered was that she had prayed.

Even though she hadn't talked to Hayden in awhile, her motherly instinct helped her to understand that something had to be wrong if God had impressed upon her to pray, even if it required waking her at an unusual hour in the morning. The thought was enough to allow an uneasiness to settle in her heart as well as a gentle pain to realize that her son may not be okay.

"Violet?" she turned to see her husband Ted, coming up behind her. She smiled as she placed a hand over his as it rested against her shoulder.

"What are you doing?" he looked at her, sleep still clouding his features.

"Praying," she said matter-of-factly.

"At three in the morning?" he raised an eyebrow as he sat in the chair beside her, reaching for her hand.

"Yes, at three in the morning. You should still be in bed."

"As should you." He smiled, sighing wearily. "It must have been an important prayer if it caused you to awaken at three in the morning."

The smile faded slightly as she nodded. "Yes. Very much so." She bit her lower lip as she looked at her husband, silently amazed thirty-seven years later that God had blessed her with such an amazing husband. "Hayden." It was enough for her husband to understand instantly. "I just woke up with this immediate, overwhelming sense to pray."

Ted nodded in somber understanding, "I had the same earlier this afternoon. I didn't want to say anything to you. No need to worry you over something I don't have all the facts on yet."

"You were going to call Calvin weren't you."

"Yes. I can't seem to get a hold of Hayden. You know that as well as I."

"Maybe, we simply aren't trying hard enough." She allowed a few moments of silence to settle between them. "You know, I think we've given Hayden enough space."

Ted nodded slowly, "Considering that God has placed this restless burden on my heart for my son lately, I think it is time to start pressuring a little bit. It can't hurt. I'll talk to Calvin too. He knows more than we do, always has."

Gently, she leaned forward to place a fragile hand against his worn cheek, "Just promise me you won't do anything drastic that pushs him away. I want both of my sons at my sixtieth birthday party."

Ted laughed heartily, "They will both be there my dear. I promise you, even if I have to kidnap my own son, he will be here to celebrate with you."

Violet sighed as she glanced at the clock, "Can we pray, again, please, one more time before we both go back to bed?"

"Of course." Ted reached for his wife's hand, bowing his head, taking a moment of silence to prepare his heart for a conversation with his Creator.

Violet bowed her head and closed her eyes as well, doing her best to set aside the anxiousness that had settled in her heart. There was nothing to be worried about, and if there was, there was no point in being worried, that lesson she had learned in her years of walking with God. While Ted prayed, she silently asked God to take away her worry and new anxiety, and that He would help her to remember that he had the situation under control, and that he was there, to hold Hayden close, even when she couldn't.

TEN

Carly flipped through the cable channels lazily, realizing then just exactly how bored she was. Maybe she should have kept her shifts at the hospital this week, at least work would have provided her with something to do. But after having decided that she needed some space and privacy to deal with her own thoughts and unanswered questions, she had decided it would be worth while to take some time off from work as well.

But all that was proving to do so far was leave her abandoned with the aged television and it's poor cable stations, and her raging anger and frustration. Angrily, she changed the channel again, this time pausing long enough to take in the football game. He hadn't even tried to stop her. And what little fight he had put up hadn't amounted to anything heroic. Where was the husband she needed, the knight in shining amour that he was supposed to be, her protector, her best friend? But he was no longer any of those.

She had wanted him to put up a fight. Wanted him to make a scene, to beg and to plead for her to stay, tell her how much he loved her and missed her and that no matter how difficult things were they would find a way to work through them.

But he hadn't. He had move out of the doorway and watched her leave without saying a word. Apparently she didn't matter any more. Apparently, she wasn't worth fighting for. That thought alone brought the fresh batch of tears as she buried her face into the pillow. They were surely headed for a divorce.

A divorce that she had decided she didn't want. She didn't want to raise this child on her own, she wanted this baby to grow up with two happily married parents who were there for him or her every waking moment. Not just mom on weekdays and Dad on weekends. That wasn't the life she had dreamed for her children.

Leaving Hayden, even temporarily, had allowed her to realize one thing. She still did truly love him and missed him more than she had ever fully realized. It was one thing to be living in the same house as the man you were having difficulties relating to, but it was a complete other to be separated, no longer with him, to at least feel his presence in the house somewhere.

But just because she had realized that she still loved him, that she wanted her marriage to work, didn't mean that all of the problems were instantly solved. Things were going to take a lot of work, maybe even professional help with a counselor.

She was about to change the channel again, when her phone began to vibrate. Cautiously she picked it up, a slight hope rising that maybe it would be Hayden calling, asking her to come back home. But when Lacey's name displayed in her caller ID window, she sighed, a strange sense of relief washing over her.

"Lacey!" she attempted to sound upbeat and cheerful.

"Hey you, hadn't talked to you in awhile, and finally found some time. What's new with you?"

"A lot." Carly sat up to rest her head against the headboard, glancing at the digital clock sitting beside her on the nightstand. "You have some free time this afternoon?"

There was a slight hesitation, "No, I don't. Are you wanting to get together?"

"Yeah. I have a lot of things I need to talk about." Carly stood to begin gathering her things.

"Does it work to meet at the park?"

"Yes, I'll meet you there in what, thirty minutes?"

"Thirty minutes should work, if I'm not there right away just wait around for me. I'll see you then."

"See you then." Carly hung up and grabbed her car keys, checking to make sure her hotel key was still in her purse. It would be good to see Lacey, to talk through all of her thoughts and the real circumstances of her marriage, and her newfound pregnancy, something she still wasn't sure how to handle or deal with.

But as she walked out of the door, something nagged at her, something she couldn't quite place. She had always talked to Lacey, about everything. This shouldn't be any different. But for the first time in eight years, she felt the need to maybe hold back, to keep this from Lacey.

She shook her head as she merged with traffic. There was nothing to be concerned about. Lacey had kept her secrets unquestionably for eight year now. She had proven her friendship. There was nothing to be concerned about, Lacey was one hundred percent, completely trustworthy.

An instant smile swept across Carly's face as she spotted Lacey Peterson standing to wave at her. Eagerly, she made her way across the park to embrace a hug from her best friend. "It has been too long!" Carly sighed as she pulled away from her friend. It had been almost a full month since she had been able to actually sit and talk in person with Lacey, her best friend since college.

Lacey batted her long black lashes as she repositioned her purse strap that had slid to her elbow, "I know! God, I couldn't wait to finish that interview so I could get here!"

"Interview?" Carly fell into step with her, headed towards the ice cream stand.

"Oh yeah, an interview with Nick Venther." Lacey smiled as she reached for her single scoop vanilla cone, "He's become quite popular all of a sudden, and the network wanted to do a feature interview with him for their highlight spot during intermissions."

"He's popular because he's an outstanding goalie." Carly didn't pay attention to hockey, but being married to Hayden Alterson, she happened to know who was who in the NHL world.

"Yeah, sure, but we're not here to talk about hockey, how is everything with you!" Lacey's eyes widened with the possibility of excitement.

Carly shrugged, silently wondering if she should share her new piece of information. She usually told Lacey everything, Lacey knew everything about her, even her deepest secrets. For days now she had been contemplating talking to someone, to admit the secret she had been keeping to herself, to talk through some of her thoughts. To tell someone, someone who would be able to help her reason and think through, give her the opportunity to express every newfound fear and uncertainty. With a deep breath, she blurted the words, "I left Hayden and I'm pregnant."

Lacey stopped walking as soon as she heard them. She stood there, looking at her, unable to say anything, finally, she rested her hands against her face, "What?"

"I left Hayden, and I'm pregnant." Carly laughed lightly as she took in her friend's expression. Pure shock.

"Wait, you're seriously telling me you left Hayden?" Lacey repeated again, this time coming to stand directly in front of Carly. " And you're pregnant?" When Carly only nodded, Lacey asked, "Does Hayden know?"

"No." Carly made herself answer. "He doesn't."

"Well, why not?" Lacey took a step back, frustration replacing the shock.

"Because," she grasped for an answer, "I don't want him to know yet."

Lacey bit her lower lip, "So how long have you known?"

"About a week now."

"A whole week and you haven't said anything to your husband."

"Well what exactly am I supposed to say to Hayden, Lacey? The two of us can't speak to each other without screaming, he's never home, and if he is we completely ignore each other." Carly felt the anger and resentment beginning to rise, and within seconds every fear and thought began to gush out of her mouth, "What kind of position is that to bring a baby into Lacey? Hayden and I are on the brink of divorce and you want me to tell me husband that I'm pregnant?"

A strange look came to Lacey's eyes as she turned to walk towards a park bench, sitting down, she looked up at Carly, "So, what made you decide to leave Hayden, with you being pregnant now."

Carly sighed, struggling to explain exactly why she had, "It's only temporary, I needed to remove myself from those circumstances, to think through my thoughts and gather myself a bit. I took some time off work too."

"So," Lacey pursed her lips, hesitating to ask her next question, "Does this mean your getting a divorce?"

Blinking back tears, Carly sat down beside her friend, "I don't know. We haven't talked about it, I had thought of bringing it up to him awhile ago, but now that I'm pregnant..." she let the thought fade into silence.

"So as of a week ago, you were planning to tell Hayden you wanted a divorce, but now that your all of a sudden pregnant, you're planning to what, stay with him? Tell him and hope that you two can work things out?"

"I know it sounds overwhelming, and impossible, but the more I think about it, the more I don't want a divorce, Lacey. Hayden and I have just been in a really rough spot since the miscarriage, and I, I love my husband." The tears splashed against her now warm cheeks, "I love him Lacey, and I want to fix things."

Lacey rested an arm against the top of the bench, "A baby just won't magically fix things you know."

Carly leaned back to look at her friend. This wasn't what she had expected from Lacey. She hadn't expected a friend who seemed more interested in the fact that she was planning to divorce her husband, than trying to help her reason through this sudden crisis that had overwhelmed her life. "What are you saying Lacey?"

It was then that the same strange expression clouded Lacey's features. Nervously, almost as if to provide a distraction, she began digging through her purse, pulling out her phone, "You know, Carly, I have to get going, but, listen, I'm sure you will manage to work everything out. And I know I've seemed a little bit extreme, but I am one hundred percent happy for you and Hayden. Congratulations!"

Before Carly could even think of a response, Lacey was already gone, becoming a blur against the crowd of training athletes running past her. Deciding that she was in no hurry herself to be getting home, she continued to sit there, watching the birds peck nonchalantly at the ground.

For the first time since she had heard the news, she allowed the tears to spill freely, finally refusing to hold them back. She wasn't even supposed to be pregnant. The doctors had told her, reassured her a thousand times that there was no way medically she could become pregnant. And out of pure paranoia she had started on the pill. Yet, despite the assurances, and the pill, she was pregnant.

How could she possibly go through yet another pregnancy? She had wanted children since she had been a little girl. All she had wanted was to someday grow up to be a mother. But she had never imagined that she would miscarry, that the opportunity to finally meet the little being growing inside of her would be stripped away. It hadn't been fair. It wasn't fair. She had wanted her first child more than anything in the world. Had loved it before she had even been able to physically hold it.

Now, here she was again, pregnant, with no guarantee that this pregnancy would endure a full term. Dr. Monroe hadn't voiced the thought yet, but she knew he had intended for her to gather the point. This pregnancy would eventually be high risk. Silently, she looked to the sky. How could God have allowed this? Especially considering that her marriage seemed to be falling apart. Lacey was right. A baby wouldn't magically fix things. A baby held the power to make everything worse.

As she finally stood to pick up her purse and tuck her phone away, she noticed a missed call from Mandy. She would eventually have to talk to her, she couldn't simply keep ignoring her. Her sister-in-law knew where she lived and eventually she would be dropping off her kids while she went to work.

But Mandy didn't understand. Their previous conversation had confirmed that much for Carly. While she had been finally relieved to admit that things weren't okay between her and Hayden, she now felt even more agitated.

Mandy had the perfect husband, the perfect marriage complete with the perfect children. Her life was constantly together and synchronized to resemble a happy family, a family who had everything they could ever want. What a family was supposed to look like. Mandy simply couldn't understand what it was like to despise your own husband, to be hurt and neglected. She couldn't possibly understand that the Hayden she lived with, was not the same Hayden presented in public, or around his brother.

Mandy would never support her decision for leaving Hayden, even if only temporarily. Once Mandy learned that she had actually gone through with the subtle threat of leaving, she would have to endure another of Mandy's "come to Jesus" talks.

Mandy would never understand. She needed someone who would support her, help her to figure out what to do, where to go, who she could turn to for help. But after a week, she was feeling lost, like a fish out of water, she had no idea what to do or where to begin. But she needed a plan. A plan would give her something to focus on, something to go by. She needed something to follow until she could pull her life back together, even if only for awhile.

Although she was lonely, she had no regrets. Absolutely none. Leaving Hayden was for the best. She simply needed time, more time. Time to think, time to process and plan. Nothing was being accomplished with her sitting around crying.

But even more difficult was the realization that she would eventually have to tell Hayden about the life that she carried. And that, was something she was completely unprepared for.

ELEVEN

Carly was pregnant. The thought pounded its distraction as Lacey attempted to focus on the interview she was trying to piece together. In shortly two hours she would be at the Ashton Arena, home to the Winnipeg Jets, who were hosting the game against Phoenix, where she would see Hayden. The simple thought of being able to finally see him tonight excited her, but at the same time, knowing that she harbored a secret that could change everything brought about the sudden frustration and fear that had overwhelmed her.

She loved Hayden. Had since the first time she had met him. Even though she had had to risk everything and destroy a friendship in the process, she had finally decided it was time to make him hers. Everything had fallen into place according to plan, had turned out greater than she had imagined, except for this.

Despite the wonderful promising news that Carly had moved out, it was a complete opposite emotion to have learned that Carly was planning on trying to make things work with Hayden. Hayden was a man of morals, regardless of the fact that he had involved himself in an affair. If he found out that Carly was pregnant, he would without a second thought end things and return home to Carly, determined to work things out.

The anger began to pound as she closed her laptop, how was it even possible that Carly was pregnant in the first place. She had been a wreck since her first miscarriage, which had ultimately ruined her marriage. Carly had forfeited her right to a faithful husband. Hayden hadn't exactly kept it secret that he wasn't receiving the attention he deserved from his wife. Yet, he had to have been sleeping with her.

That single thought alone illuminated her anger. Apparently his attention wasn't singly divided to her. He was sharing it between the two of them. It wasn't a secret that she was jealous of Carly. Had been since the start. But she had grown tired of being Carly's friend long ago. In fact, it was becoming exhausting to keep up with her faked friendship.

She herself was a woman who deserved what she wanted. And if a married man was willing to ruin his marriage to be involved with her, he was fair game. Hayden deserved to be with her. Carly was nothing compared to her. Gorgeous and talented with a professional career that allowed her to spend time with Hayden wherever he went. Not to mention that she understood his profession more than Carly did.

But regardless of how much she deserved and could provide Hayden, he would never see it that way. But to her advantage, Hayden didn't know Carly was pregnant. And from the sound of things, Carly had no intentions of telling Hayden any time soon, which allowed her plenty of time.

A few days from now, she was to meet with Hayden again. It would allow her to test the waters, to ensure everything she had convinced herself of. It was time she had decided, to present her ultimatum. She herself hadn't planned to present the ultimatum immediately, but considering Carly's newfound pregnancy and sudden willingness to make their marriage work, she had to. If she didn't ask Hayden to leave Carly once and for all to make everything right, she would never have the chance. Hayden would be more likely to agree fully believing that there simply wasn't any reason why he shouldn't leave Carly. After all, his marriage was in complete shambles.

And by the time he learned that Carly was pregnant, it would be too late. Hayden would be with her. The divorce would be in process, and he would be fully committed to her.

TWELVE

"Uncle Hayden!" four-year-old Anders threw himself against Hayden's legs, clinging to them tightly, forcing Hayden to lean back into the doorframe.

"Hey, bud, can you let go for a second please?" Hayden couldn't help but smile as his nephew released his grip, standing back to smile broadly at his uncle.

"You're here!" he half shouted.

Hayden chuckled at the remark, "I am indeed little man! Were you waiting long?"

"Forever!" Anders dragged the word out to emphasize the eternity he had endured waiting for his uncle to arrive for supper. "I have to show you! Come on!" he gripped his Uncle's hand as he pulled him with all his weight to begin leading him into the kitchen.

"Hayden!" Mandy smiled as he followed Anders in. She wasted no time asking, "Where's Carly?" Silently, he gulped. How was he going to explain that Carly had moved out? There was no simple way to explain it, especially with the small Anders standing beside him, curiously also beginning to wonder where his Aunt was. Carefully he constructed the lie, "She was called into work at last minute. They needed another nurse in emergency."

Mandy looked as if she was about to question him, but Anders drew the attention back to him, "Look, Uncle!" Hayden glanced down to see a piece of red construction paper with a coloring page mounted on top of it. "Hey sport did you color that?"

Pride beamed from Anders eyes as he bobbed his head viciously, "Yah, all by myself!"

"It looks good Anders, really good! You even managed to stay in the lines this time." He reached out a hand to ruffle the mop of hair that sat atop Ander's head.

Mandy set down the knife she was using to slice some tomato, "Calvin's outside barbecuing. You should go help him."

He glanced out the patio door to see Calvin flipping burgers, "Yeah, I don't need him burning down the house." He made a face at Hannah as he passed the table where she sat coloring. She giggled as she looked up at him, "You going to cook me a hotdog?" she asked.

"Sure, I'll make sure to burn it for you." He winked as she twisted her face, "Gross!" she shook her head, "Cook it good okay? I don't like burnt food!"

"But that's my specialty." He mocked as he reached to playfully tug on one of her pigtails.

"Hey!" she swatted at his hand as she threw her crayon to the table.

Hayden laughed he tugged again, this time backing away to say, "I"ll see you in a little bit okay? Your dad could use some help." He pushed the patio door open to smile at his brother, suddenly slightly nervous.

"Bout time you show up!" Calvin sarcastically reprimanded as he took a step back, a flame leaping from the grates.

"You got everything under control out here?" Hayden watched as Calvin threw down the lid.

"Course." Calvin nodded his reassurance, "Not at all." He laughed as he pulled the cook's apron over his head. "Here, these belong in your hands." He handed the tongs to Hayden.

"I saw the fire engine pass me on the freeway, thought for sure they were headed here." Hayden joked lightly, leaning against the railing of his deck to take in the early summer sunset.

"Almost had to have them come here." Calvin took a seat in the deck chair, stretching his legs before him. "Been awhile since we've actually gotten to talk! How are things going!"

The question caught Hayden's attention, "Why?" he asked.

"Just wondering. Like I said, haven't really had the time to talk to you lately. You disappear after games, won't answer your phone, Carly's either working or doesn't know where you are."

Hayden busied himself with turning burgers, adjusting the temperature of the grill, suddenly concerned as to where Calvin might be heading with this conversation, "I've just been busy Calvin. I get home and Carly wants me to go here or there, get the groceries, fix the sink. I lost the charger to my phone too awhile ago, haven't had time to pick up another one."

It never ceased to amaze him how easily the lies came sometimes. Hayden wasn't sure what his brother was getting at, but it was enough to set him on edge. Attempting to hide the slight panic and concern that was developing he turned to look at his brother, "What have you been up to?"

Calvin shrugged, "You know, everything. Music concerts, parent teacher conferences, hockey games, practice, being a dad and family man. I find enough to keep me busy." He paused as he took a long sip from his Pepsi, "Dad called the other day, wanted to know if we were still going to be able to make it to Mom's birthday party."

Hayden had completely forgotten about his mother's birthday. He absolutely wanted to be there, "Of course. You still going to be able to make it."

"Wouldn't miss it for the world." Suddenly, a strange expression crossed Calvin's face, "Where's Carly?"

Did everyone have to notice that Carly wasn't with him? Maybe it had been a bad idea to come over to his brother's for supper once he had called with the invitation. He should have known better, that they would ask about Carly. Anxiously, Hayden flipped the burgers again. In past years he had kept secrets from Calvin, but as they had grown older, their brotherly bond had strengthened, to the point where they confided in each other as men did. Besides, Calvin would have to find out sooner or later anyway.

"She left, Calvin."

There was a moment of complete silence before Calvin leaned forward in his chair, "She left as in?"

"She left me. She is no longer living in the house." Hayden wasn't sure how to quite describe the fact that she had left him. Usually "she left me" only meant one thing.

Calvin set his Pepsi down, "Why?"

Hayden shrugged, "Things haven't exactly been okay between Carly and I. There's been a lot of fighting, distancing; we simply don't talk any more. I came home yesterday to find that Carly had packed a few things and was leaving for awhile."

"Is this a permanent thing?"

"No, just a temporary thing. She needed some time or space, however you want to look at it. Carly will be back when she's ready." To ease his brother's mind he added, "We've always managed to work through things, you know that."

A long, heavy sigh escaped as Calvin rubbed his chin anxiously, "Hayden, you should have said something."

"What was there to say?" Hayden leaned lazily into the deck railing. It wasn't his brother's business how his marriage was. His problems were his own.

"You could have said that things weren't okay. Mandy could have talked to Carly, we could have prayed for you. Well we still can."

There it was again, Calvin's need to bring God into everday life. Hayden had abandoned the God that Calvin seemed to enjoy a relationship with. For Hayden, God simply didn't fit in. God didn't control anything. There was no use for him. Hayden had gotten everywhere in life on his own, without the help from God. Besides, if God had really cared he wouldn't be in this mess, and God wouldn't have taken their child.

"Yeah, you do that." Hayden offered the simple phrase that had saved him many times from Calvin's religious speeches. In the midst of his current circumstances, he didn't need to hear how badly he needed Jesus.

"Hayden, I'm sorry, but you know, God will use this for the better. Maybe this space apart will help you both to realize what's truly important, and that you still love each other." Calvin nodded confidently. "Does Mandy know?"

"No. I told her Carly had picked up an emergency shift at the hospital last minute."

Calvin nodded in understanding, "No need to get her alarmed. I can talk to her later tonight once the kids are in bed. No need to ruin the fun of everything."

Hayden couldn't believe how laid back his brother was being about this entire situation. Usually Calvin was ready to fix things, give you the answers to your problems, the solutions to everything. Instead, he was simply sitting there sipping away at his Pepsi. Hayden was thankful for it, but it was still strange.

As Hayden ignored a look from his brother, he busied himself heaping the burgers and hotdogs onto the platter Mandy had obviously left outside for them.

"Oh good! The foods done!" Mandy walked out onto the deck, taking the platter away from Hayden, "Did I interrupt something?" she asked, looking between the two of them.

"No, no you didn't." Calvin smiled at his wife, "We were just about to bring that platter in; I'm next to starving!"

Thirteen

Calvin reached for the remote, turning down the volume to gain his wife's attention. "Hey, I was watching that." Mandy raised her eyebrows as she reached for the remote.

"I know." Calvin smiled as he stretched his arm away from Mandy's reach. "We need to talk about something."

Mandy sat up, bending one leg beneath the other as she turned to evenly look at her husband. "About what?"

"Hayden and Carly."

"Is something wrong?" Mandy instantly became concerned, her voice rising.

"Shh." Calvin reminded her of their sleeping children. "It could be serious."

"Could be serious? Calvin what is going on?" Mandy slid closer to her husband, instant panic mixing with her sudden concern.

Calvin scratched his head, waving a hand to emphasize his own confusion and uncertainty about his brother's latest news, "Hayden said Carly has moved out, only temporarily." He added hastily.

"What?" Mandy's eyes grew wide with surprise and shock, her mouth hanging open.

"Carly left Hayden." Calvin repeated shortening his previous announcement to bare briefness.

"Well, I heard you, I just didn't think she would actually go through with it!"

Calvin shook his head "Wait, you knew?"

Mandy sat back, biting her lip, "Well, last week when I visited her, she had mentioned that she thought it would be best if she and Hayden separated for awhile, so she could think, but I didn't actually think she would go through with it."

"Well, she did." He sighed as he leaned into the couch.

"And only temporarily?" Mandy continued, sitting back to look at him, "Calvin, it's not, could be serious, it IS serious!"

"Well, I wouldn't say that." Calvin looked at her evenly, attempting to say the right things to help his wife calm down a bit.

"Calvin, be honest with yourself." Mandy rested an elbow on top of the sofa, "She won't be moving back in."

"Now, don't jump to such harsh measures. Some marriages require that one or the other leaves for a while, to help start on fixing and restoring their marriage." Calvin could think of a few couples that he had known who had to resort to such measures, and they were still together.

"I know." Mandy crossed her arms as she wiggled her way closer to her husband, snuggling against him. After a few moments of quiet, she finally said, "Did you know things were this bad, between them, I mean."

Calvin rested his chin against the top of her head, "No. In all honesty, I mean, I knew something wasn't quite right, every couple has their share of arguments, that's all I assumed it was."

"Are you going to tell your Parents?"

The question shocked him. He hadn't even thought of his parents, "I don't know." He stammered for an answer. Should he tell them? His mother had called the other day strangely enough Hayden hadn't even crossed his mind. "I don't even think it's my place to tell them. Hayden needs to."

Mandy accepted the answer, sighing as she glanced at the t.v. for a moment. "You know," Mandy turned to look at her husband, focusing on what he was about to say, "Hayden is a completely different person." A strange sense of sadness overwhelmed her. She fully understood what Calvin was talking about, she just hadn't heard the words physically said aloud until that moment.

"He's just a completely different man Mandy. I don't even know my own brother any more."

Gently, she reached for his hand, "I know." She smiled softly, "We all change though."

Calvin looked at her seriously, "I don't think this change has been for the better."

"I know." The smile faded. "Calvin, is there a reason as to why Carly left, even temporarily."

Calvin bit his lip, "He didn't say why."

"Does she know?" Mandy asked carefully.

"About the rumors?" Calvin asked.

"Yes, about the rumors. I haven't seen Carly at any games lately, and I haven't seen her at any of our events, or at our lunch dates with the other wives." She bit her lip, "I doubt she would know, about them."

"Because if she knew about them, she would suspect or question Hayden." Calvin sighed restlessly. "Considering how much Hayden has changed, considering the things I have been hearing, Mandy, I'm not saying he is, but I'm not sure he isn't either."

"Involved in an affair."

He could only bring himself to nod, "But I'm not sure yet. I'm giving my brother the benefit of the doubt. They are simply rumors at this point. And that is what I will choose to believe."

"Does Hayden know about the rumors." Mandy asked next.

"I'm sure." It was impossible for him not to know about them. Men talked, locker rooms were natural breeding grounds for genuine male conversation. "Mandy, all I am saying is that we need to keep this between us for now and pray. Pray for him and for Carly."

Mandy nodded her agreement, and after a long pause, kissed him goodnight before heading up the stairs. As he sat there alone on the couch, watching the Discovery channel flash before his eyes, he silently couldn't shake the doubt that taunted him.

He had to give Hayden the benefit of the doubt, but Carly moving out wasn't a sign of anything good. Something was seriously wrong with his brother's marriage, and as his brother, Calvin felt deep concern. He had to keep talking to Hayden, let his brother know he was there if he ever needed to talk. Allow his brother to understand that no matter what, regardless of what he had done, they still loved him, but most importantly, he had to pray. Continue to pray that God would work in his brother's life, and that no matter what, God would remind his brother that he was indeed still loved, and forgiven.

Fourteen

Hayden leaned his head against the headboard, struggling to catch his breath, as a deep frustration and annoyance began to overwhelm him. Normally, time spent with Lacey proved to be nothing short of amazing, but tonight, it was the furthest thing from it. Instead of feeling a sense of physical release, he only felt more tension and now, frustration.

"What are you doing?" Lacey propped herself up on her elbow, her long hair flowing over her shoulders to spill onto the sheets.

He sighed as he released his grip on his pants, it had been a stupid idea to think that he would be able to just get up and leave right after having slept with her. Lazily he sighed as he rested against the headboard again. "Nothing." He sighed again.

"Are you okay?" a strange, puzzled look crossed her face as she looked at him.

Was he okay? The irony of the statement caused him to chuckle lightly. No, he was not okay. He was sitting here beside a woman in a hotel bed that wasn't his wife. He had just slept with a woman that wasn't his wife, the woman that had singlehandedly helped him to ruin and devastate his marriage. Carly had moved out, temporarily as she claimed. His brother was suspicious, while his career was slowly slipping away from him. Was he okay? No, he was not okay, but instead he said, "I'm fine. Why?"

Taken aback by his sudden edge, Lacey sat up, gathering the sheet around her body. "You just seem different tonight, that's all."

He shrugged lightly, scrambling to come up with an excuse that would satisfy her, "Just stress, you know."

She nodded slowly, "I guess. I mean what with you being so close to the playoffs and needing to win three games, the pressure must be there." Slowly, she came up beside him, placing her hands on his broad shoulders. Gingerly she began to work her fingers into his muscles, "A little time spent with me though, should relieve all of that stress." She whispered into his ear.

Something within him silently snapped as he slid away from her, "Don't." he heard himself say.

"Don't what?" Instantly, she became defensive, her eyes narrow with both surprise, shock and confusion.

He threw the sheets back, getting out of bed to reach for his pants. Tugging them on, he glanced over his shoulder to see her getting up to reach for the dress she had previously been wearing. Eagerly, he tugged on his shirt then reached for his socks, as he glanced about the room for his shoes. The instant need to be suddenly be away from her, outside of this room began to suffocate him.

"Hayden?" He turned to see Lacey standing in the doorway of the bathroom, a loose bathrobe hanging around her petite frame.

When she had his full attention, she said carefully, "If I said anything to upset you, I'm sorry."

The intense need increased, and he felt his chest begin to tighten. She had nothing to be apologizing for. Perhaps that was what bothered him the most. Being with her, with Lacey, hadn't bothered him before. Only twice, the first time he had slept with her, and then the second. But after that, the enjoyment and pleasure that accompanied the sense of freedom from a depressing situation had eased and erased all of his guilt, at least, until now.

Uneasily, he ran a hand through his hair, "You have nothing to be sorry for." The words left a bitter taste in his mouth as he instantly wondered if he truly meant them.

She glanced at the floor before looking up at him again. "Are you leaving?" A childlike fear and uncertainty clouded her eyes.

He reached for his hoodie and baseball cap, "Yeah, yeah I am." He sighed as he tugged the hoodie over his head, "I just, ah, have somewhere to be, and I'm tired." The two excuses sounded lame as they bounced off of the walls surrounding him.

Lacey took a few steps towards him, crossing her arms to rest against her stomach. "Okay." She nodded, "When will I see you again?" she stood directly in front of him now.

Uneasily, he took a step back, "I don't know. I'll call you." He stepped past her, narrowly avoiding her as she started to lean in for a kiss, usually their way of saying goodbye as they temporarily parted until their next meeting. But tonight, the idea only drove him to an instant panic.

As he rushed out into the hallway, he leaned against the wall a deep sigh finally escaping his lungs as he suddenly remembered how to breathe. Hurriedly, he slipped on the sun glasses he had stuffed into his hoodie pocket, glancing up and down the hallways to make sure no one had been in the hallway to witness his rushed exit from their room. Seeing no one, he attempted to calm his breathing as he headed back down the hallway towards the elevator.

What was wrong with him? He shook his head, attempting to clear some of his suddenly distracted and rushed thoughts. Where was the cool, calm and collected Hayden Alterson that could spend a whole night with Lacey, with next to no thoughts about what he was doing or about Carly. He had never second guessed his actions up until now or even taken them into consideration.

As the elevator doors opened, to ground floor, he searched the now completely abandoned lobby, no one save for a few like himself were up at this hour. Silently thankful, he headed across the parking lot towards his BMW. Anxiously, he unlocked his door then slid behind the wheel. Slamming his door shut. He leaned into his seat, feeling some of the tension beginning to release.

Angrily he slammed his hand against the steering wheel, attempting to create a release for his frustration. It shouldn't be this way. Things shouldn't have come this far. He shouldn't have started the affair to begin with. Lacey was a pass time, a way to have a bit of fun and escape the depressing life he had been enduring.

But now, now Carly was gone, and lately that seemed to be all that mattered. Carly hadn't been his constant thought for months. Where she was, or how she was had never occurred to him. Lacey had replaced Carly, both physically and mentally. Shortly after he had started sleeping with her, he had found he couldn't stop thinking about her. All he had wanted was to be with her, and for the past few months he had done anything and everything to ensure that he could be with her as much as possible, without anyone finding out.

Now, he thought of Carly constantly. Wondering where she was, where she had gone, what she was doing, if she was working. He could easily find out the answer to any one of his questions, but she had asked for space, and he would give her that. She deserved at least that much from him.

It was then that a depressing and frustrating sadness flooded through his being. He hadn't done right by Carly. He hadn't been the husband he had wished and always wanted to be. Instead of loving and supporting her, he had only managed to hurt her.

Suddenly, for the first time in months, all he wanted was to go home and wrap his arms around Carly, to hold her close and simply be with her. But Carly wouldn't be at home. She wouldn't be there for him to embrace comfortingly. A slight ache filled his heart as he acknowledged also a reality that he hadn't understood until a few days ago.

He would have to go home, where he would be completely alone. The thought left a bitter terrifying loneliness to settle in the pit of his stomach.

As he merged with traffic, he decided that there had to be a way to make things right, without Carly finding out about the affair. A part of him knew he should tell her, be honest about everything, but that at this point would only do more damage than good.

But how to begin making things right, escaped him.

FIFTEEN

Ted Alterson easily recognized the outline of his son blurring easily with the setting sun as he pulled into the gravel entrance. The high school had shut down long ago, after the school had been forced to merge with a few remaining smaller schools in the area. As a result one high school had been built, but the football field and track had remained in fair condition, with some minor upkeep from school board members. Occasionally, the old field was used as another practicing facility, but most days, it served as the perfect running track for his sons to keep in shape. No one knew that they loved to run here when the weather allowed it. His sons were free to run in peace without people pestering for autographs or people shooting for a single picture.

It was a marvel to him as he got out of the car to approach the track just how idolized his sons were. How they were living the life he had given up years ago, never accepting the offer that had been presented to him. He had played seriously in the AHL, had had his own dreams of playing professional hockey for the rest of his life until he was no longer physically able to. But then, God had called him into ministry, and he had never looked back.

Now, years later, his own two sons were not only playing in the NHL, they were famous, but not for their looks or how much money they earned, famous for their talent, and character and how they managed to play together. Silently, he stood by the track, waiting for Hayden to take notice of him. It didn't take long, as Hayden slowed his pace to try to make out who was standing beside the track, having to distinguish if it was a family member or a member of the surrounding public. Once he was finally close enough, Ted waved, smiling broadly at his son. It had been too long. Too long since they had had a simple conversation.

"Hayden." He wrapped his son in a warm embrace, ignoring the fact that he smelled and was sweating.

"Hey Dad." Hayden's chest heaved as he fought to develop a normal breathing pattern. "What are you doing here?" he swiped at a train of sweat that begun to drip beneath his nose.

"Wanted to see you. Tried at the house, but you weren't there. So I figured I'd try here." He took in his son, the broad shouldered six-foot man who had once been a staggering toddler. With his mother's distinguished, direct eyes, and straight black hair he was a reminder of just how much things had changed in the past years. "It's been awhile son."

A look of guilt washed over Hayden's face as he gulped for air, "I know Dad, I know. Things have just been busy, and that's no excuse either." Hayden had always made time for his parents, had always made sure to take at least a day if not a few hours out of his week to visit his parents, talk with them, tell them about how things in his life were falling together. But lately, he had avoided his parents.

"That's not your fault son." Ted stepped onto the track to stand evenly beside his son. "Big night tomorrow."

"Yeah." Hayden sighed as looked out across the field, "Against Phoenix. It'll be a hard one that's for sure. I leave in about an hour."

Ted nodded slowly, "That it might. That it might, but you've seen hard before and persevered through it. You always have, and what you haven't succeeded in winning you've always learned something valuable. Built character. Just focus on playing your best, keep your head in the game, focus and everything will be fine."

A silence settled between them, as Ted silently struggled to find a lead in for the real purpose behind his visit. Granted, it was always wonderful to visit his sons simply because he could, but sometimes, as a parent, his children required visits of purpose. "We're hoping to see you at the party."

Hayden looked at him, a strange smile broadening on his face, "Yeah, I know. And I will be there. Calvin mercilessly reminded me. How is mom doing?"

"Fine, although she hasn't been sleeping well." Ted scratched at the unshaven scuff that had built about his chin.

A look of concern filled Hayden's eyes, "Why hasn't she been sleeping?"

Ted wondered silently if he should say it, there was no point in telling a lie or beating around the bush, "Well, she's been waking during the night with the overwhelming sense that she needs to pray."

Furrowing his brow Hayden remarked slightly sarcastically, "In the middle of the night?"

"Yes, in the middle of the night."

"What's she praying about?"

"You." Ted watched as his son instantly moved into defense mode. Anything that regarded to God in any form even prayer instantly caused Hayden to back away, often ending conversations.

Hayden took a step to distance himself from his dad as he glanced at the ground. "She doesn't need to be praying for me."

The words inflicted a delicate, wounding sorrow for Ted, "How have things been going Hayden?" he forced Hayden to meet his own gaze so that he could actually determine Hayden's true reaction. Hayden's expressive eyes had always revealed the truth, and even though he had become better at hiding his true feelings, he had always worn them on his sleeve.

"Things are fine dad." Hayden matched the direct gaze for only a few seconds.

Things weren't fine. "How's Carly?" Ted asked next. He had developed a love for his daughter-in law over the years, treasuring the blessing that God had placed in his son's life. He couldn't have personally imagined that God would bring such a wonderful young woman into his son's life.

"She's good. Mostly working, haven't really seen a lot of her though."

Ted could tell there was some honesty to the comment. "You being away from each other so much with work and such doesn't help to foster communication any."

Hayden's sigh warned Ted that he was pushing the limits, and that he was losing patience. Not wanting to anger his son and push him away, he backed off, silently praying that God would grant him the peace to let things rest at least for now. Lightly he moved into lighter conversation, enjoying the time with his son. It didn't take long until Hayden was laughing along with his dad, sharing glory moments and fun events from his recent games and the experiences they had brought him.

Finally, Hayden had to depart, not wanting to be late for his flight with the team. Hayden said his goodbyes, thanking him for coming out, reminding him to tell Mom to get some sleep and to wait to pray for him in the mornings if she absolutely had to.

As Ted drove home he couldn't shake the feeling that had settled over him. There was something that he was trying far to hard to cover up, to keep hidden away. Ted knew his son all to well, and despite Hayden's attempts to make him believe that everything was fine, he knew better. The matter troubled him. But he didn't know what was troubling his son, and without knowing, there was no way to help him. He would have to talk with Calvin, pry about in a fatherly manner to see if he could at least find some answers to the questions that were building.

Sixteen

Lacey Peterson hurried to splash the cool water against her face, welcoming the refreshing feeling that tingled through her cheeks and chin. Anxiously, she took a final glance in the mirror to make sure she hadn't smudged her make up. Finally confident that she looked put-together, she opened the bathroom door and discretely made her way down the hallway.

Shaking her head to clear it a bit, she headed into the staff room. Wearily she took in the smell of stale donuts and burnt toast, the smells that she usually didn't notice suddenly horribly sensitive. Easily they assaulted her nose as she headed towards the abandoned coffee pot, wondering just how fresh the black brew was.

Finally deciding that she was to desperate and in too much of a hurry to make a fresh pot, she poured herself a cup and crossed the room to take a seat on the worn out sofa. Eagerly, but hesitantly she took a sip, cringing as the coffee burned its way down her throat, leaving her tongue tingling.

Sighing, she leaned into the couch, closing her eyes. For the past few days she hadn't felt like herself at all. Even though she was getting a good night's rest she was still waking up in the morning feeling drained of the energy that she required to make it through her fast paced days. She had tried everything from exercising more, to eating more fruits and vegetables, limiting her caffeine, hoping the problem could be resolved by improving her diet. But more and more now, she was finding herself requiring at least four cups of coffee to make it through a single day.

She had even resorted to stealing quick naps in between her breaks, finding that that helped a bit, but not much. She had even had to start taking Tylenol in an attempt to dull the pain of the headaches that seemed to plague her as well. As she sat there holding her cup of coffee she hated to admit to herself that maybe she should take another tablet, but what good would it do? Nothing seemed to be helping her any more.

Thoughts of making a doctor appointment had crossed her mind, but she had decided to give it a few more days. After all, it couldn't be entirely serious. Her job involved high stress accompanied by exhaustion. It wasn't uncommon to be plagued with a headache every now and then. And jet lag was often a contributing factor to being over tired. It was all related to her work, it had to be.

"Morning Lacey!" Marjorie Simmons flaunted a smile with tilting hips as she paraded her way through the door, her own coffee cup in hand.

Silently, Lacey cringed. She had been doing well all day, her goal to avoid Marjorie as much as possible. Now, she would be stuck in this break room for a good hour while she gabbed away about nothing in particular, which would only worsen her currently developing headache.

"Morning Marjorie." Lacey attempted to sound somewhat enthusiastic, but the dullness in her voice was enough to catch Marjorie's full attention.

"You okay?" Marjorie placed a hand on her stuck out hip, asking the question instantly, skipping past the usual light conversation.

Lacey seriously contemplated lieing to her, but she knew by her complexion alone it was obvious that something wasn't quite right, "No, I'm not." She began piecing together her vague answer, "I just have a headache, haven't felt myself lately."

"Tired?" Marjorie leaned against the counter, her mint green wad of gum passing back and forth in her mouth. Lacey could only bring herself to nod, just the word made her want to curl up into a ball and close her eyes.

Marjorie chewed thoughtfully, "Tired and you have headaches." She glanced at the coffee cup, "Obviously it's not because your lacking caffeine."

"No, it's not the caffeine." Lacey agreed with her plainly.

"You know," Marjorie studied her carefully, "My sister had those same two symptoms when she found out she was pregnant." She snapped her gum angrily, a small chuckle escaping, "But that's obviously not the reason with you, you don't even have a boyfriend, darn, you ain't even seeing any body!" she laughed heartily to herself.

Silently Lacey smoldered. Marjorie Simmons knew everything about everyone from who they were sleeping with to what toothpaste they brushed their teeth with. It still frustrated her that the woman seemed to know everything about her when Lacey hadn't told her anything to begin with. But it was a comforting thought to know that Marjorie didn't know everything about her. She didn't know about the affair with Hayden Alterson, one point against her. "No Marjorie, I am not pregnant." She stated clearly, emphasizing as strictly as possible.

"You sure?" Marjorie's gaze searched Lacey's expression, pressuring her to give up anything, something that would be of a hint to her, something that might reveal something she didn't know.

"I am sure." Lacey stood then, clutching her cup firmly. "I would know if I was pregnant, and you would certainly know Marjorie, being the queen of gossip that you are."

Marjorie only laughed, her maroon curls flopping against her head, "I would know wouldn't I."

Lacey wanted to physically assault the woman, so self centered, selfish, and nosey, the few characteristics that she had never liked in a person. Who was she to think that she would have the right to know whether or not she was pregnant, not that she was or ever would be. Deciding it was best to remove herself from the situation, she faked a polite smile, chuckling pathetically along with Marjorie, "Well, I have to get back to work, I think I've taken a long enough break, I'll see you later Marjorie."

"Oh sure enough, can't imagine how much work you have, seeing as how Blaine seems to give everything to you." The sly remark struck another nerve with Lacey, as she was sure it was meant to.

She laughed again, her smile fading slightly. She wasn't going to offer a comment. There was no point in stooping to such lows with a creature like Marjorie. Silently fuming she made her way back down the hall towards her own office, Marjorie's comments still nagging her, singing their way through her thoughts.

Angrily she plopped into her computer chair, not caring how unprofessional it may have looked. Pregnant. It was a ridiculous thought. So what if Marjorie's sister had had the same symptoms, it didn't mean anything for her personally. A woman could have headaches and feel tired and not be pregnant. She was on birth control anyway, and they had always used protection. There was no need to even consider the fact that she might be pregnant.

She pushed the thought from her mind as she forced herself to focus on the paperwork before her. She would give herself one more week. If these same symptoms continued after a week, she would schedule an appointment. There was no possible way or sense in thinking she could continue her job in a state like this. It just simply wasn't healthy. She needed to be fully healthy in order to meet the regular demands of her job.

Huffing a strand of hair away from her face she mumbled angrily to herself. "Pregnant. Oh, that woman!" She simply just wasn't pregnant.

It was simply a ridiculous idea.

Seventeen

Lacey exhaled slowly, carefully, shaking her head. No, it simply wasn't possible. She tossed the stick into the garbage, reaching for the second box she had purchased. Eagerly she ran to her kitchen, where she poured herself another glass of water. Anxiously, she chugged it, desperation encouraging her. Hoping that the sense to relieve herself wouldn't take as long as they had before, she curled up on her couch where she impatiently began flipping through a magazine.

An hour later exhausted of trying to keep herself distracted, she rose from the couch, dashing to the bathroom. Picking up the second box she shredded her way to the test within. After completing the instructions for the second time around, she waited impatiently for the results. In dismay, she stared at the results, positive, two tests had deemed positive. She was pregnant.

Listlessly, she walked out to her bedroom, sitting down on the edge of her bed. Pregnant. What was she supposed to do with a pregnancy? She couldn't have children; she didn't want children, never had. Her career wasn't meant to include children, a baby would be a nuisance, keeping her from continuing with the career she loved.

Confused and overwhelmed she pushed the free strands of hair away from her face. Pregnant. What was she supposed to do? Angrily, she fell back onto her bed, still clutching the stick that beamed the simple but true result. Angrily she shook it, hoping by some shred of uncanny luck the result would change. When it remained the same she sat up, suddenly feeling horribly ill.

A millions thoughts of new worries and fears began to torment her. Causing a strain of tears to slide down her fair cheeks. Clenching her fingers into a fist she turned to pound her relentlessly against her comforter. How could she have let herself get pregnant? Hadn't she taken all of the necessary precautions? Hadn't they done everything right?

This pregnancy didn't just affect her; it affected Hayden as well. What would Hayden think? How would she tell him? But most importantly, how would he react? The questions swirled and tossed and chanted their woes while she curled up into a snug ball and allowed herself to cry.

Finally when she had exhausted the last few tears, she sat up slightly to reach for a Kleenex, feeling the self pity and slightly depression beginning to suffocate her. She wasn't suddenly worried any longer about how this baby would affect her personal life, but more concerned about how it would affect Hayden. Anxiously she allowed his name and face to fleet through her thoughts, when suddenly, a new thought began to beg for attention.

Slowly, it began to brighten and form, with a small glimmer of promise beginning to unveil. Eagerly, she sat up, pulling her comforter to her chin. She wasn't just pregnant with any baby. She was pregnant with Hayden Alterson's child.

Willing she admitted the facts to herself. She was pregnant with a baby that was the product of an affair. Up until recently, she was technically still single, having provided Hayden with a benefit relationship only. He wasn't tied to her in any other way save for a sexual relationship. Sure, they were friends, not best friends but still, a friendship of which they could hold a normal, personal conversation.

Recently, her desire for more than just a sexual relationship had been only wishful thinking. Angrily she sat up, already unsure that their relationship was going to endure, considering Hayden and his suddenly changed attitudes and personality. Lately he had seemed bored if not annoyed with her presence. She had thought for any man that a sexual encounter would be a pleasurable experience, but now it seemed as if he was bored with that too.

He was still in love with Carly, that much she was capable of seeing. But with a marriage in shambles surrounded with frustration and hurt, just how much longer would he be willing to hang on? How much longer would he be willing to remain and tolerate the woman who seemed to enjoy making his life miserable?

She herself was better for him, actually *loved* him. And now, more than ever her chances of convincing Hayden to leave Carly seemed all the more real. Hayden would have to leave Carly to be with her. She was pregnant with his child after all, there had been and was no one else. Hayden didn't know that Carly was pregnant yet, all she had to do was tell him of her own newfound discovery; and being the morale man that he was, he would leave Carly to make things right with her.

Maybe, perhaps this baby, this pregnancy was the best thing that could have happened. She smiled slowly. The final touch to making Hayden realize and understand that she loved him and that there was no other woman for him had finally been provided for her. All she had to do now was tell him, talk to him.

Now was the time, especially if Carly was considering fixing her marriage. Soon, Hayden would know that he was going to be a father. That he was finally going to have what he wanted most in the world and that she was capable of giving it to him.

Hayden was finally going to be hers.

Eighteen

Calvin glanced up the ice searching for his brother, but unable to find him, and being pressured by the defensemen skating towards him, passed the puck back to Simone, who drew back for an even slap shot. Calvin stood completely still as he watched the puck fly through the air, players moving and dodging until it met Carter Thatcher squarely. He reached with his glove to snatch the puck out of the air, holding it for the whistle.

Granted, it hadn't been the best slap shot, but usually, a shot from Simon found it's way into the net. But they weren't against just any goalie, they were up against Carter Thatcher, whose team was as equally driven to advance to round two. The Ottawa Senators weren't far behind the Jets, having endured a ten-year cup drought of their own. As the whistle blew, he skated a small circle to calm himself down. They still had ten minutes in the third, plenty of time to pull of a goal if they absolutely wanted to. But tonight wasn't a matter of want; it was a matter of need. They needed to force overtime so they could use the extra time to achieve a win.

"Cal." Hayden's chest heaved as he stopped to stand beside his brother, "We need a goal."

Calvin used his gloved hand to wipe at the sweat streaming down his nose, "We don't need to figure out how to get another goal, we need to figure out how to get it past Thatcher."

"We have thrown everything at him." Hayden glanced ahead to the goalie who had left his crease to skate a few paces.

"Not everything." The whistle blew and Calvin skated to the offside faceoff, where Hayden now stood face to face with the opposing center forward. Eagerly, he gripped his stick, watching as Hayden focused on the blue circle before him. As soon as the puck left the referee's hand, Hayden crossed the blade of his stick left to right, then left again, winning the faceoff.

Calvin caught the puck and skated backwards to observe the situation. Hayden was working his way straight to the net, placing himself in front of Thatcher, as he looked to his left, he saw the left wing approaching him, skating back towards the boards, he passed the puck to Alex, who fought to get past the right wing. As Calvin turned to avoid a hit, he watched as the right wing managed to steal the puck then slap it down the ice back into their zone.

Circling to get past the center forward, he watched as Nick Venther passed the puck ahead to their defenseman, Brooks, who passed it ahead to Hayden. Hayden worked his way down the ice, passing the puck back and forth with Alex as he went. Finally, Calvin managed to position himself in front of the net. Fighting off the defenseman as legally as he could. Using his stick he slapped the ice, "Here! Here!" he yelled, as Hayden circled behind the net.

He had to reach slightly, but the puck touched his stick, and with the twist of his wrist, he managed to pull it towards him. Taking a few seconds to fight off the defenseman working for the puck, he turned sharply to send the puck flying. Hoping it would somehow find an open piece of net.

But as he turned to look fully, he saw Thatcher slide across the crease on his knees to place a glove over the puck. A sigh of frustration and defeat escaped as he skated away from the crease. Nothing was working.

It was then that he heard the crowd suddenly erupt. Turning to see what had caused the commotion, he took in the sight of his team crowding around Hayden and the opposing center forward, Carl Ansley. Carl was yelling some insult or another at Hayden. Alex was doing his best to hold Hayden back, but it wasn't enough as he broke free.

Calvin watched as the gloves fell to the ice, Hayden's fists clenched, bringing on a fight. Carl and Hayden circled each other, testing to see who would make the first move. Finally, Hayden threw the first throw, meeting Carl's jaw evenly. But Carl, recovered quickly, sending a throw of his own capable of leveling Hayden with little effort.

Hayden fell backwards onto the ice, laying there for a moment before finally standing up, blood running from his nose. Calvin heard the referee announce the penalty, watching as the referee escorted him to the penalty box.

A sudden frustration mounted in Calvin as he watched Hayden take a seat on the bench behind the glass. This penalty would allow Ottawa to score a goal. Four on five was not their strong point. With eight minutes left on the clock, he could only hope for the best. The desire to move to round two of the playoffs ignited a passion to accomplish anything.

Sighing to push away his frustration and focus solely on what needed to be accomplished, he skated ahead to take the responsibility for the faceoff. Staring at the red circle before him, he saw the puck fall in slow motion, saw it hit the ice, but as he moved the blade of his stick across the ice, he realized it was too late. Carl Ansley had won the faceoff.

Defensively he retreated into his zone, watching to see where the puck would be sent. If he could intercept a pass, they could still end up back in the opposing zone to score a goal. But their forward dropped the puck as he skated ahead for his left wing to pick up. With speed and precision, he sent the puck to the right, using the boards to bounce the puck straight to their forward, who stood in front of the cage.

With little motion, he caught the puck, skated behind the net, and without looking, turned to shoot. The puck sailed passed Nick Venther's glove to hit the meche behind him. The siren erupted and the crowd became deafening.

Hayden ashamedly skated out from the penalty box, headed straight for the bench. Ambers immediately seated him, substituting Justin Camt. Calvin also accepted a seat on the bench, beside his brother.

"Let it go." He said as soon as he had a chance. He watched the play resume, while hockey jerseys skated past their bench.

When Hayden didn't say anything in return, Calvin decided to watch the remainder of the period. Finally, the siren erupted again to announce the finish of the period. Hayden was the first off the bench, skating past anyone who was waiting for an interview.

Curiously, Calvin hurried to follow him into the dressing room. Angrily, Hayden stripped his jersey and threw it against the bench. "Hayden." Calvin said with enough sternness that let Hayden know he was serious. "Let it go."

"I can't!" Hayden turned to face him now, pure anger illuminating his face. "I shouldn't have. I shouldn't have fought!"

"Then why did you." Calvin stood back as a few of his teammates began to fill into the room.

A strange look crossed Hayden's face as he turned to sit down on the bench. "I can't do this any more." Even though Calvin was sure the words hadn't been intended to be heard, he had caught them.

"Can't do what?" Calvin looked at his brother, wondering what in the world had possessed him. He was making no sense, none whatsoever.

"Nothing." Hayden said quietly as he leaned down to begin unlacing his skates, realizing that someone had been paying attention.

Understanding then that Hayden was finished with this conversation, Calvin returned to his own locker to begin undressing. But while he joked around with his teammates, struggling to shrug off their loss, he couldn't help but wonder about his brother. It was completely uncharacteristic of him to fight. But truth be told, he hadn't played very well tonight. Not the normal Hayden Alterson that the league had become adjusted to. Something was bothering his brother, enough to seriously be throwing off his game. And this close to the playoffs, they couldn't afford to lose their star player.

Hayden would have to figure out whatever was going on, but what he had to figure out, Calvin hadn't the slightest idea although a few things were beginning to come to mind, however, he didn't dare say them aloud for fear they would suddenly be true.

Nineteen

He had to pull himself together. If he didn't, he risked losing everything. His entire team was depending on him. They didn't say it and Ambers certainly didn't voice the thought, but he knew it just as well. Considering tonight's loss they would have to win two in a row. The odds were in favor for them, that much he did know. But if his game continued to fall apart like it had tonight, he risked blowing those favored odds for not only himself but his teammates.

Frustrated he climbed behind the wheel of his car, slamming the door shut as he rested his head against the headrest. Closing his eyes, he listened to the rain silently beat against his windshield. He wasn't simply frustrated with his game. If she hadn't approached him before the game had started, he would have been fine. He had managed to push every troubling thought from his mind, pulling together his game mindset. But then she had appeared,

"Hayden." She had walked right up to him, ignoring any concept of personal boundaries.

"What?" he asked, glancing up and down the hall to make sure no one could see them, any minute anyone could walk out of a dressing room or down the hallway. He already had rumors circulating about what might be possible. He didn't need anyone to solidify them as actual fact.

"Will I still be seeing you tonight?" the hazelnut brown eyes that usually flaunted her flirtatious and fun nature were filled with something he couldn't quite place.

"You know not to be talking to me Lacey." He backed away, "I have to get dressed."

"Wait!" grabbing his arm, she used enough pressure to get his attention, "I need to talk to you."

"Not now!" he had whispered, harshly enough so that she would understand. "I can't be seen with you outside of an interview. You know the boundaries we created. Respect them." He turned to walk away then, headed towards his dressing room. Thankfully, she hadn't followed him, but her approach and nature of the conversation had been enough to distract him for the entire night.

His actions had proved his frustrations and distraction. He hadn't built his reputation based on fights as some men in the NHL did. He preferred to be known for his leadership characteristics, his smart play, and simple talent that meshed together with that of his brother. Together, they were able to create plays that allowed goals.

He also made it a point to avoid the penalty box as often as he could, so whenever a fight presented itself, he had made a habit of turning away. With a sigh, he leaned forward to buckle his seat belt. He still had to meet Lacey, something he wasn't exactly thrilled about at the moment.

As he pulled out to merge with the traffic, he heard his cell phone begin to vibrate. Knowing better than to pick up his phone while driving, he decided to ignore whoever was trying to get a hold of him. But when his phone vibrated again, he picked up the phone, taking a quick glance to catch the name, Calvin.

Tossing the phone back onto the passenger seat he leaned into his own seat in an attempt to get comfortable. Calvin knew something was wrong. His brother knew him better than anyone, including his own parents, which meant that Calvin would be pressing for answers soon. He was a man who needed answers to questions; he had always felt the need to fix a problem as soon as he had identified one. Even if he wasn't sure what that problem was, he would figure it out. He would have to tell his brother something, but what he didn't know. Calvin didn't exactly believe in just anything, and Hayden was a horrible liar.

The irony of that thought suddenly bothered him. He was a terrible liar, yet somehow, he had managed to pull of a three-month affair, an affair that his wife hadn't even detected a slightest hint about. By now he had thought for sure Carly would be wondering, questioning where he was and what he was doing, but then again, her lack of interest in what he was doing showed just exactly how much she cared about him.

The thought irritated him and he felt the familiar frustration beginning to itch within him, the frustration with not only his wife, but with Lacey as well. But while the frustration tormented him, he was reminded of the complete feeling of loss he felt. Loss for his inability to solve the problem he had created; to find a way to repair his broken marriage. To end his affair with Lacey and leave her behind as if nothing had ever happened. But that was wishful thinking. Even he was willing to admit that much to himself.

Over and over again the problem tormented his already exhausted brain. It wasn't a matter of him not wanting to end the affair, but rather how to end it. For far too long already he had become bored with her company, what had once been exciting and distracting was now only annoying and mundane.

The fact was simple. He didn't want to sleep with her. But he was sure once he was back in that room he would feel the pressuring temptation, the toying thought that one more experience with her could be amazing. No man was capable of backing away from a stimulating experience someone like Lacey could provide.

Again he reminded himself of the fact that his relationship with Lacey was simply sexual. Nothing more. There wasn't the same connection and attachment with Lacey as there was with Carly, or had been. But lately, before Carly had left him, Lacey had seemed to be trying to change that.

Longer and longer he found himself laying in bed with her, bored out of his mind while she chattered away with aimless conversation. Mostly about her life and problems she was facing. He had ignored most of it, nodding and agreeing in as few words as possible, but still audible so that she didn't catch on to his disinterest.

But tonight, he wasn't sure what was going to take place. All he knew is that she wanted to talk to him, about something serious. Even though she hadn't said anything to indicate such a conversation, he had picked it up from her strange behavior around him, the different pleading that had gleamed in her eyes.

Finally, the hotel came into view, and hastily, he turned into the parking lot. Unsure that anyone hadn't been following him, he reached behind the passenger seat to grab the plain, dirty baseball cap and fan baseball jersey he kept on hand. It wasn't exactly the kind of attire anyone expected a professional hockey player to be wearing, especially one such as himself. The general public knew he wasn't a baseball fan. His life served as an open book for the public, something he wasn't exactly thrilled about.

Silently, he crossed through the lobby, keeping his gaze level with the elevator doors. In a few short moments he was walking down a hallway, headed towards room 408, where Lacey would grant him entrance. A single, quiet knock resounded lightly down the hallway, but Lacey opened the door before anyone with a nosey character could peek with their prying eyes.

"Hayden." She forced a smile as he walked past her into the room. There was a different feel about the atmosphere, a feeling of foreboding clinging to him. Usually, it was an energy of fun and excitement that met him.

"Hey." He greeted pathetically as he watched her sit down on the edge of the bed. She was fully clothed, not even in her lingerie, which she usually, flirtatiously wore. "What's going on?" he asked carefully, not caring to beat around the bush any further. She had distracted him, had helped him to lose his focus which had lead to a game loss. She had approached him out of context and was currently wasting his time; she should get to the point.

"Hayden, I know it was wrong of me to approach you before the game, and I'm sorry, but I really needed to talk with you. It's not exactly something you should be sending through a text message or delivering in a phone call." She met his gaze for a moment before glancing back at the evergreen carpet.

Attempting to keep his frustration in check, he leaned against the wall, "What did you need to talk to me about? I can't stand here all night Lacey." He could see that she was put off by his sudden harshness, but she deserved it.

"Hayden, I'm pregnant."

Hayden felt his heart skip a beat as he continued to glance at the carpeting. He couldn't have heard her right. "Pregnant?" he asked as he looked up at her now.

Lacey shifted uncomfortably, "I hadn't been feeling well the past couple of weeks. At first I thought it was a flu, that it would go away, that I was just working too much, the stress was getting to me. But I was still feeling sick, nothing that I'm used to. Someone made a passing joke that I could be pregnant. But I took it seriously. I took the test yesterday afternoon before I flew here, and it was positive. I'm pregnant."

Twenty

His thoughts swirled in a vicious torrent. Instantly, he began to shake his head. It wasn't impossible. He had used protection, had known something like this was a possible risk. He hadn't wanted to take any chances. "No, you're not." He defied this time aloud.

"I am." She reached into her purse to reveal a pregnancy test, which she held out to him, "I kept it, in case you wouldn't believe me."

Hayden held the test with disgust as he glanced at it long enough to read the positive result. Angrily, he threw it onto the bed beside her, "How could you have gotten pregnant?"

Instant hurt and confusion flashed in her eyes, "Keep your voice down!" she hissed, "And what do you mean how could I have gotten pregnant? I didn't exactly accomplish this on my own!" Tears brimmed and threatened to fall as Lacey stood up, crossing her arms against her chest. When Hayden remained silent, she took a shaky breath, "Hayden, what are we going to do?"

The question assaulted him like a slap to the face. What were *they* going to do? *They* weren't going to do anything. It was then that it hit him, the full realization of what she was driving at. She was pregnant, pregnant with *his* child. He held even responsibility to this sudden situation. He had fathered a child, with a woman who wasn't his wife but rather his mistress, a child who was the product of an affair.

Instant alarm and panic rose combining with his frustration. "I don't know what we're going to do!" he spat barely above a whisper.

Lacey nodded slowly, finally daring to say, "I gave it a lot of thought and consideration.... I think you should leave her Hayden." Lacey looked at him evenly now, tears running down her fragile cheeks.

The words hit him harder than her first announcement had. Slowly he struggled to understand and grasp what she had just asked him. The anger he had been fighting suddenly flashed through him. Did she actually have the audacity to ask him to leave his wife, simply because she was now suddenly pregnant? He allowed his mouth to hang open. What exactly was he supposed to say to that?

Moments ticked by slowly in agonizing silence. There was nothing to say to her obviously undignified request. Leaving Carly had been an option months ago, even more recently weeks. But now? Now he had arrived at the understanding that he didn't want to leave Carly. Suddenly horribly uncomfortable and needing the chance for some air, he licked his lips impatiently and walked towards the door, turning to face her.

"Lacey, I need some time, and some space." He finally said, the familiar panic pressuring his chest.

She sighed with a hint of impatience and disbelief, "I know what I just said had to be overwhelming, but Hayden, we need to talk about this. It's not just simply going to go away."

He shifted impatiently, scrambling for an answer. He had to get away. Had to get away from this woman who had suddenly ruined everything for him. "Lacey, I need to think, time and space to think about things, about us, you, Carly."

A strange expression crossed Lacey's face, "Carly?"

"She is my wife Lacey. We are still legally married, regardless of the current circumstances. Whatever I decide affects her. I not only have you to think about, but her as well." He rationalized determinedly.

She half scoffed at him, "Well, regardless of what you think, Carly has nothing to do in this situation. This is about you and me, and this baby."

Her referral to her pregnancy as an actual baby overwhelmed him, made the situation too real. "I can't deal with this right now." He threw his hands in the air.

"Well you're going to have to deal with it at some point Hayden."

"Well that point isn't now!" he shouted the words with as much harshness as he could muster. She needed to understand, understand that he wasn't prepared to deal with all of this all at once. He needed space, time to think about everything she had said, to put together a plan.

Through the fear, uncertainty and obvious hurt melting across her face, she said simply, "Hayden, I love you. And I want to put together a family for this child. I need you Hayden."

The words took his breath away. She loved him? She wasn't supposed to love him, she was simply a sexual being for him, an escape from the miserable life that confronted and oppressed him in his own home. He didn't love her. She didn't *need* him, wasn't supposed to *need* him. But before he could piece together a response, she continued, "I'm sorry Hayden, I really am. I shouldn't have put all of this on you, especially right before the playoffs. But I do love you, and this is a reality now. We share a child, whether you like it or not. And we need to be responsible for this child.

"I understand that you need some space, I shouldn't have been so angry, I didn't expect to resolve all of this in one night. I'll give you the time and space your asking for, but eventually Hayden, I will need an answer."

A silent thankfulness swelled amidst the horror, fear, anger and frustration that had suddenly built. She was giving him time and space, that much he was capable of comprehending. "Time and space," he nodded simply, "I need to go, Lacey."

She only nodded, her tears mixing with the hair that had spilled against her face. She looked so pathetic simply standing there, a look of defeat haunting the eyes that usually held so much ambition and determination. Before he walked out into the hallway, he realized and acknowledged a truth that crushed him. He hadn't just hurt himself; he hadn't just ruined everything for himself; he had done the same to Carly, and now to Lacey, a woman whom he had once called friend.

He had taken advantage of a friendship and at the same time, ruined it. But it wasn't all completely his fault. She had thrown herself at him, had made it known that she was more than happy to oblige in helping provide him with an escape from a marriage that was suffocating him. She had taken advantage of him just as much as he had her.

As he walked to his car, he acknowledged that everything had suddenly changed. But how, he wasn't quite ready to acknowledge or comprehend, but in time, he was sure he would feel the devastating affects. This wasn't something that could stay a secret, not like his affair. This newfound pregnancy was now an evident proof of his affair, a testimony to his unfaithfulness. He couldn't hide her pregnancy, eventually she would begin to show and people would begin to wonder; they would have questions.

And Lacey wouldn't stay quiet for long. It was obvious to him now that she intended for more in this relationship than pleasure. She wanted him, wanted him in a way that he could never be for her. He was not in love with her.

Lacey was a woman accustomed to getting what she wanted, and when she didn't, the consequences were devastating. Just how long would Lacey stay quiet? Just how much time and space did she intend to give him? Surely, it wouldn't be long. Eventually she would begin to push for answers. Answers he didn't have, and probably wouldn't have for a lengthy amount of time.

Twenty-One

Violet stood back to admire her birthday cake, carefully placed on the table in the middle of all the snack foods. She loved birthdays, even if it was her own. While others her age complained of growing older, wishing they didn't have to refer to themselves as *old*, she was completely happy to do so. To her, there was nothing wrong with growing another year older. She enjoyed the phases life brought her, and year sixty-five was one to look forward to.

"Grandma!" Hannah came running out of nowhere to wrap her arms around her grandma's legs, "Happy Birthday!" she squealed happily.

Violet laughed heartily as she reached down to pick up the girl that was smaller for her age, "Thank you sweetheart." She buried a kiss in the tangle of brown waves that her mother had pulled back with a pink headband.

"Grandma!" Anders appeared now, in front of his mom and dad, holding a white envelope. "I made it." he held it forward proudly.

Setting Hannah back down on the ground, Violet bent carefully to accept the crinkled envelope decorated in random crayon scribbles. "Thank you Anders!" she admired the childish gift, feeling a small place in her heart glow with pride. Her grandson had made her a birthday card, and she knew exactly where she would be placing it!

"Happy Birthday Mom." Calvin stepped forward to embrace her, holding her close against his big frame.

"Thank you Calvin!" she smiled as he pulled away, suddenly wishing that he would have allowed the embrace to last for a few more seconds. There was something special about the way a mother and son could share an embrace.

"Violet," Mandy came forward next, pushing her son Anders out of the way delicately, "Sixty five and still as young as ever!" she winked as she allowed for a quick, but light hug.

"And don't you forget it!" Violet giggled as she took a moment to take in the family standing before her, proof of the blessings the years had brought her.

"Hello!" Ted came up behind her, also wrapping his son in an embrace, "Where's Hayden?" he asked, after he had welcomed and admonished over Ander's card.

Violet glanced around then too, suddenly aware that Hayden still had yet to arrive. While she was surrounded by true and wonderful friends, her family was what mattered the most to her. Her birthday just wouldn't be complete without Hayden and Carly. "Have you talked to him lately?" she looked at Calvin and Mandy.

Calvin hesitated to answer, but Ted responded quickly, "He promised me he would be here, when I last talked to him."

Mandy nodded her head in agreement, "I talked to him earlier this morning, and he said he would be here. I'm sure he's just running late." She rested a hand on Violets arm reassuringly. "We all will be here; give it a bit more time."

"You're right." Violet nodded, once again aware that she still had others to greet. "I need to excuse myself for a few moments, help yourselves." She waved her hand towards the bowls full of snack mix and various chips.

Fifteen minutes later, she randomly glanced away from a friend to see Hayden making his way towards her. Immediate excitement overwhelmed her as it had been far too long since she had last seen him! "Hayden!" she exclaimed, pulling him into a tight and warm embrace. "It has been too long, son!" After a few minutes, she finally realized she had to pull away, reluctantly doing so.

"I know mom, I've been busy." He smiled warmly as he looked around the crowded yard, "You obviously know how to throw a party."

"Well," she sighed, "I didn't expect this many people. Your father mostly planned the whole thing." She took a moment to take him in, studying the broad shoulders and boy-like smile that reflected the child-like character that still existed at times. Yet past the smile, and past the dancing eyes, she could see the mystery of something darker. Something deeper and haunting reflecting carefully masked misery.

It was then that she realized Carly wasn't with him. "Where's Carly?" she asked quietly. She watched as the panic clouded in his eyes, but he shrugged nonchalantly, "She had to work. Last minute, they're under staffed."

Violet wasn't sure that she could believe what he had said, but decided to ignore the comment, she had to if she was to enjoy her birthday. "That's too bad, I was looking forward to seeing her."

"She was just as disappointed." He agreed quickly, far to0 quickly.

Violet decided not to push the subject, or question it, but the matter still troubled her. "You finally made it!" Calvin clapped his brother on the shoulder, smiling broadly, and for a single, fleeting moment, she wished she had her two small boys again. As a mother, regardless of how proud she was, there were still moments when she wished she could go back, to hold them again as tiny infants, watch them take their first steps, nurse their scrapes and bruises. Watch them develop and become the men they were today. Instead, the memories were tucked away preciously in the deepest chambers of her heart.

"Carly?" Calvin raised an eyebrow, looking around the yard as if Carly was away grabbing a cup of punch. But there was something strange about the way he asked about her, almost hopeful, inquiring.

Hayden only shook his head, not even providing the answer he had given his mother. Instead he pushed the conversation forward, moving his brother away. He knew that eventually, later, the large crowd of gathered people would eventually dissipate, leaving the brothers with their families to enjoy a good visit with their parents.

Violet watched the two walk away, watching as Hayden suddenly reached into his pants pocket to pull out his cell phone. A strange expression clouded his face as he hastily tucked it back into the pocket where he had pulled it from. As she turned to visit with an old friend who had stopped to with her a happy birthday, she attempted to push the troubling thoughts from her mind, but couldn't quite do so fully, the matter constantly nagging in the back of her suddenly loud conscience.

Twenty-Two

Calvin left the crowd of men he had found himself surrounded in. Although it had been several years since he had been drafted, the people who his parents called friends were still impressed with the idea and fact that he was a professional athlete in the NHL. For more than an hour he had been forced to listen to his "glory" plays, the best moments, the best fights, how he had overcome challenging games against equally skilled hockey players. But now that they had successfully positioned themselves in a playoff position, the talk had seemed to turn to what games they had already won against their first round opponent, Washington. How to win games, the tactics, the mindset to develop and endear as his own had all been given as advice.

But the advice, although he knew it came from well intentions, wasn't helping to ease the pressure he felt. Everyone seemed to have an opinion as to how to win games, how it was important and an amazing opportunity that the Jets were finally in a playoff position after a fifteen-year drought. Not to mention the talk that had surfaced more than once, how devastated fans would be if they lost.

Having heard enough, he excused himself politely, silently searching for Hayden. Mandy found him first however, "Calvin, I really think we should be going." She pointed to the sleeping Anders, curled up soundly on the porch swing, his sweater serving as a pillow. He sighed, it had grown late, Hannah was nowhere to be found, but he knew she would also be tired, and developing an attitude within a few short minutes. Mandy's eyes were pleading silently, and he recognized just how tired she was as well.

He smiled as he wrapped an arm around her waist, pulling her towards him gently, "I know." He breathed into her hair. Savoring the brief moment of peace, he whispered into her ear, "I need to find Hayden first."

Mandy sighed as she rested her head against his chest, "Alright, but, after that, we leave."

"Okay." He nodded as he kissed her softly, "I'll find you later. You may as well go back into the house with Mom."

She pulled away, wrapped her arms around herself as if to ward off the sudden chill that had settled around them. Anxiously he glanced at the sky. Black threatening clouds had left the night sky starless, the porch light and a small fire providing the only light in the small yard, accompanied by a streetlight. How he was to find Hayden was beyond him, but the pressing need he felt to talk to his brother pushed him forward.

Finally, after walking through the entire yard, he found Hayden, standing in the back yard by the sidewalk, his phone pressed to his ear. The closer Calvin came, the more he could hear, although Hayden was keeping his voice low, too low for him to pick up anything being said. However, the tone was clearly audible, a low even tone that sounded frustrated and almost desperate.

When Hayden finally realized that Calvin was approaching, he rushed through a goodbye, tucking his phone back into his pocket. "You're being missed up there you know." Calvin nodded towards the front yard.

"Yeah, I know." Hayden shifted uncomfortably, "I had to make a call."

Calvin nodded, "I won't ask to whom, you can relax."

Hayden's shoulders dropped then, a sigh of relief escaping him. After a few moments of silence he looked at Calvin, "Some birthday party. I didn't know Mom had that many friends."

"Neither did I. But she's a popular woman you know, active on all the church boards." Calvin wasn't about to tolerate the pointless small talk much longer, but he endured it for a few more moments. Finally, he pushed to the main reason he had sought out his brother. "How have you been?"

Again Hayden shifted uncomfortably, shrugging, "All right I guess."

"You seem to be holding up well through the playoffs." Calvin continued, watching his brother's red hoodie shift with his shrugging shoulders.

"Yeah, I don't have quite so much on my mind any more." Hayden smiled dumbly, he wasn't convincing anyone.

"How's Carly?"

A long, sad sigh escaped from Hayden as he stared off into the distance, watching a firefly float its way across town, "I haven't talked to her since she left. I half expected her to call, but she hasn't. So I called her tonight, left a voice message. But I doubt she'll call back."

A moment of silence settled between them, "She'll talk to you when she's ready Hades, you just need to know when to be there, and when to listen rather than speak."

Hayden nodded slowly, "If she ever comes back." He kicked at a random pebble, "I miss her Calvin. More than I thought I ever would. I was half glad you know, when she left. And yet, I'm more miserable than ever. I love her, I do. And I miss her like crazy. I haven't been the best husband. But I can improve that, if only she'd give me a chance. I just want her to come back."

Calvin studied Hayden then, realizing that his was the most candid his brother had ever been. Hayden was a man who kept things to himself. Even as a child he had never admitted to what was bothering him, which had left everyone frustrated. He had never given a glimpse into how he was feeling, or what he thought about a matter. Now, before him, stood a very vulnerable Hayden.

"Maybe Hayden, you should be telling Carly that, rather than me." He said slowly, carefully.

With a strong gulp Hayden struggled to control himself, "I don't deserver her, not after what I've done." He said barely above a whisper.

Even though he was sure Hayden had only meant it for himself to hear, Calvin had heard it, "What do you mean Hayden?"

Realizing that Calvin had heard him, Hayden shook his head, "Nothing."

Slightly confused, but suddenly seeing a window of insight, he said carefully, "Hayden, regardless of what you have done, Carly will forgive you. You both are in a world of hurt, that only God can ease, you need each other Hayden."

Sudden anger filled Hayden's eyes, "you don't understand what I have done. She'll never forgive me, which is why I won't tell her."

Calvin was suddenly lost, but found himself saying, "Carly may not forgive you, but God will Hayden. Turn to God and he will comfort you. Nothing is impossible with our God."

"Your God." Hayden spat angrily. "Not mine." He turned away then. "I have to go."

"Hayden, I'm sorry." Calvin started after him, realizing he had pushed the conversation too far. "Please, don't leave. Mom will be wondering."

"I have to go." Was all he said again as he climbed into his car. Helplessly, Calvin watched as he started the engine and drove off, while his mother came up behind him.

"Something is horribly wrong isn't it." she asked quietly.

Calvin could only nod, "Yeah. And I don't know what. I don't know how to help him, Mom."

She placed a hand on his arm, "Neither do we Calvin, neither do we. But we know someone who can, and he will, in time."

Calvin sighed with frustration, knowing his mother was right, but he struggled to hold his trust in the words. There was only one thing he could do for his brother, and that was to pray. It was all he had left.

Twenty-Three

A rather dull sense of hope flooded through her as she picked up her cell phone to find a missed call from Hayden. Quickly, she flipped her phone open, rushing to her voice mail. Hesitantly, she held her breath as she pressed her phone to her ear. "Carly, I need to talk to you, I miss you, please, won't you come back?" the message ended then, and Carly hurried to replay the message.

As she sat back down on her bed, a small sense of anger begged for introduction to the swirls of feelings rushing through her. It had taken him almost a month, more than a month she acknowledged, for him to contact her. It had taken him this long to realize that he missed her and that he might actually care about her? The thought wasn't exactly reassuring, Hayden shouldn't have to second guess or think about whether or not he loved his wife.

"At least he called." The thought pounded dully. A soft smile spread to her face, he had called her. He wanted her to come home! But was she ready to come home? True, she missed him, and true she was more lonely than she had ever been in her entire life, she hadn't even felt this confused after her father had left. But just because she was lonely, and missing her husband, didn't mean that all of their problems would simply be solved if she returned home.

Anxiously, she placed a hand over her stomach, silently thinking about the new concern that had been added to her already long list of troubles that had plagued her thoughts for the past month and half.

Having decided that she needed to begin piecing her life back together, while she attempted to figure things out she had gone back to work, welcoming the distraction. She had rented a small apartment, admiring the freedom she had gained, the peace that she had found in being by herself for the past weeks. Finally, she had brought herself to accept that she was pregnant. The fears and the concerns still very present, but now, a new sense of joy overwhelmed her. She was finally pregnant, her miracle baby.

A sad smile haunted her features, her miracle baby that may not be. After having accepted the fact that she was pregnant, she had brought herself to schedule her first prenatal appointment. Anxiously she had sat in the waiting room, listening cautiously for her name to be called. It had been a full year and half since she had been through this exact same process. Finally, she had risen from the chair, following the doctor down the hallway into the small room.

After a thorough examination, answering some basic questions and asking her own, she finally dared to ask the question that haunted her, "Is there a chance that this baby, won't be carried to full term?"

The OB sighed carefully, as if contemplating what to say. "The fact that you have struggled to conceive in the past, and considering your extensive miscarriage a year ago, yes, there is a chance that you could lose this baby. In harsh honesty, it's a risk with every pregnancy, although most are carried successfully to full term without worry."

The words had deflated the small balloon of hope that had swelled in her heart. Silently, she fought back tears. "But I still have a chance?"

Dr. Shanahan nodded slowly, "Yes. You do. However, it is a very serious and slim chance Carly. As this pregnancy develops I will be listing this pregnancy as high risk. For now, it is okay for you to still be working, however, I want you to cut back shifts. Attempt to limit the amount of stress in your day, avoid stressful situations. Eventually, you will be on bed rest."

The words took a few minutes to fully sink in, and as she began to process their meaning, a single tear slid down her cheek, "I don't know if I can do this again." She whispered.

Dr. Shanahan smiled sadly, "Carly, this pregnancy is a miracle, we never thought that conception would be possible for you again. You are a strong woman, a woman who deserves this child. And I personally, along with my medical staff are going to do everything in our power to help you carry this baby to full term. You need to believe that everything is going to be all right. Have to give yourself that hope again. But Carly, you also need to understand the risks and seriousness that goes along with this miracle pregnancy, which is why I told you."

Nodding slowly she wiped the tears away from her cheeks, "I know." She had known it had been too much to hope for; too much to hope for a fully healthy baby that might endure a normal safe pregnancy.

Now, sitting in her tiny apartment, she wasn't sure it was in her best interest to return home, she still wasn't fully convinced that she was one hundred percent ready to mend her marriage, while she wasn't convinced she wanted a divorce either. But the tension, the struggle and stress that attempting to mend her marriage may present, she wasn't sure it was worth putting the baby at risk., or herself.

Returning home would also mean that she would have to tell Hayden, which she had to do inevitably. Weighing all of her worries and fears, she wiped the familiar tears from her cheeks. Despite her worries and fears, the new voicemail replayed through her mind constantly. Reminding her of just how much she missed Hayden.

She truly didn't want a divorce. Had promised herself the moment she and Hayden had become engaged that their marriage would last. That no matter what life presented, no matter the challenges they faced, they would endure and persevere together. But she hadn't expected it to be so hard, hadn't expected that she wouldn't be able to have the one thing she wanted most; that a single miscarriage could change everything over night.

Even now, as she sat on her couch, she reminded herself of her parents. She had always promised herself that she would never end up like them, divorced, bitter, angry and alone. She had floundered personally to accept her parents divorce as a child, had struggled to accept what her father had done. It wasn't the life she wanted for the child she carried.

With a sigh she brought herself to the acknowledgement that their relationship had changed and evolved over the few years. She would have to accept the reality that Hayden wasn't the man he had been, and she was no longer the woman she had been previously. They had both changed, and so had their relationship. She couldn't expect the same from him as she had before. Should she return home, should she finally decide to work on her marriage, she would have to remember that things would always be different.

It would take time, and effort, and a lot of work. Counseling would be needed. She would have to insist that they needed to move things slowly. She would finally tell Hayden of her pregnancy, allow him to be part of the experience that he deserved. Allow him to be a father. It wasn't fair of her to continue keeping this secret from him.

Finally, after weighing and considering the circumstances she had replayed over and over again, she decided that she would give it a trial. Being involved in the playoffs, Hayden wouldn't be home as much, which would provide her with space, and time to herself to adjust to being back home. Slowly, as the hockey season winded down she would be able to find the time to talk to her husband again. They would need time to learn to communicate again.

As she glanced at the calendar, she acknowledged that she had paid her rent for up to five months, which would allow her to be able to return if she needed to. With a slow smile and a sense of hope and promise over coming her she stood to head to her bedroom to begin packing.

It was time to face the situation she had avoided most. Time to tell Hayden that he was going to be a father. Time to work on her marriage, the child she carried would need to be brought into a happy, healthy home.

Yes, it was finally time, time to return home.

Twenty-Four

"Lacey......Lacey!" She glanced up to see her camera man Jack standing in front of her. "You ready to go?" he asked, eye brows raised in silent question. It then occurred to her that she hadn't been paying attention, and that he had been talking to her, but she hadn't heard a single word.

"Yeah, yeah I'm ready." She nodded over eagerly, wondering whom she was trying to convince, herself or Jack. He blinked at her saying half sarcastically, "Game starts in twenty minutes, warm ups are taking place, we should get situated." She silently chided herself as she followed her team down the tunnel, she should have been paying more attention. Warm ups had already started, and she had been standing around lost in her own thoughts.

As she ran a hand through her hair to even out any tangles that may have appeared, she wondered silently just how put together she looked. It was actually amazing that she had pulled off looking this decent for the camera, considering the day she had had. Anxiously, she placed a hand over her stomach, willing the nausea that tormented her to subside. But it was pointless. Eventually she would have to schedule an appointment to see if there wasn't anything that could be done for the relentless torment.

But she couldn't make an appointment until she had talked with Hayden again. She was well known enough that people recognized her easily, even though they had to question which network she worked for, they knew she was a famous sports anchor. It would be obvious enough as to why she was visiting an OBGYN, but after that, everyone would have questions. Instant speculation would begin as to who the father was, and she would be tormented by other unending questions. She couldn't answer those questions until she had talked to Hayden.

Hesitantly, she made her way out onto the ice, walking as briskly as possible without falling to get behind the bench where she would conduct most of her interviews during intermissions or pauses throughout the game.

As she stepped into the area behind the bench, what nerve she had built up melted instantly as soon as she saw Hayden, making his laps around the ice, handling the puck as he went. Quickly, she averted her glance to spot which coach she would interview before the game, then attempted to decide whom to interview next. Would she interview the captains or random players?

She managed to conduct her first interview without any flaws or incident, marveling at how cool and collected she found herself to be, how confident. After the camera had turned away however, and the coach had walked away, the confidence and collectedness disappeared almost instantly.

Finally, warm ups ended, while players skated to center ice to line up for the national anthem. Robotically, she turned to face the flag, placing her hand over her heart in allegiance. Throughout the entire anthem, she couldn't help but sneak peeks at Hayden, who had set his jaw stubbornly, staring straight ahead. She knew instantly that he was doing his best to ignore her.

Even though she knew he had to ignore her in order to focus on the game he was about to play, it still angered her. Slightly miffed and annoyed she felt her own jaw setting stubbornly. She was after all, pregnant with his child and deserved at least some acknowledgment. As he skated towards the bench to get the final words from his coach, Ambers, she glanced away, focusing on what was happening on the ice.

Throughout the game, she cheered silently, knowing that the Jets needed to pull off a win tonight in order to advance into the second round of the playoffs. Everything was riding on tonight's game. As first and second period passed, with no goals, goalies giving their all to protect their sacred net, she cheered and gasped and booed along with the crowd, however, only loud enough for Jack to hear her.

Finally, in the last eight minutes of the game, Clavin and Hayden approached the net, Alex skating closely behind, centered directly down from the net. After a pass from Hayden, to Calvin, Calvin faked the shot, working quickly to pass the puck back to Alex, who wound back for an even slap-shot. The puck soared into the meche, allowing the siren to sound throughout the arena. They had scored and were winning with a rare one to nothing lead. Anxiously the crowd watched as the clock began to wind down, players giving their all, boards cracking with the weight of men slamming against them.

But it wasn't long until Washington managed to answer to the Jet's goal. Almost too easily, a penalty to the Jet's Eric Moddard allowed the five on four play to create a chance, with their star forward beating Nick to score. Now tied at one to one, the tension in the air became thick, Eric Moddard skating from the box with a sheepish shame drooping his shoulders.

It seemed that the game would be forced into over time, but the Jets were not to be underestimated. In the last remaining minutes, the Jet's Oscar Harting stole the puck in a defensive effort, turning to pass the puck blindly up the boards. Alex caught it, glanced ahead only long enough to target Hayden, standing alone behind the opposing defense. A strong, sure slap-shot sent the puck evenly to Hayden, who with a burst of speed skated into a breakaway. One on one with the goalie, he moved left, then right, glancing momentarily, getting closer and close. Finally, he moved his stick to shoot, faking a shot, and waiting long enough for their goalie to sail down onto his knees, sliding across the ice to where he thought the puck would be.

Eagerly, Hayden pushed the puck through the created opening, smiling as he heard the sirens erupt once again. The crowd erupted as Hayden jumped against the boards, piled by his teammates. Accepting slaps and pats on his head, he smiled broadly as he lingered amongst not only the men he called teammates but friends as well. With only a few minutes remaining on the clock, the crowd was deafening with their praise. The group of celebrating men dispersed then, to take the final faceoff position for the game that night. Finally, the clock winded down and the victory siren resounded.

The reality of the event began to sink in then. The game was over. The Winnipeg Jets had earned their right to head to the second round of playoffs after a fifteen-year Cup drought. She took in the scene, marveling as coaches hugged one another, while players smiled and hugged on the ice, slapping shoulders and laughing.

But the joy and excitement she had felt over their victorious win disappeared as she realized she would have to interview Hayden, team captain. Suddenly, she wanted to crawl under a rock, to be at any other game than here, someone else should do this interview. But she had to. If she didn't people would wonder why she hadn't interviewed the goal-scoring hero.

As she walked up to him, making eye contact to let him know she was headed his way, she read the instant disappointment and uncertainty that had filled his eyes. He had made it clear he wanted nothing to do with her. "Hayden, how does it feel to have just scored the game winning goal that has helped advance this team to round two of the playoffs?" she spoke loudly into her microphone, stretching to hold it up to his height.

He shook his head, the amazement of his accomplishment still settling in, "Amazing! I mean, we have a long road ahead of us, but to realize what we just accomplished. It's simply amazing."

He paused for a moment to wipe the sweat dripping from his face, waiting for her next question.

Almost flawlessly, she struggled to work her way through the rest of her simple, yet direct questions, all the while faking a smile and joyful attitude, knowing he was doing the same. As he skated away, she noted the suddenly stiff shoulders, and set jaw. Previously he had been over-joyed, excited, and overwhelmed by his small yet monumentous feat. As he skated to head back down the tunnel to the dressing room, he was confronted by his teammates, whom he smiled and laughed with, but yet remained guarded.

As she wrapped things up for the evening she couldn't help but feel a sudden despair. This wasn't how she had imagined things turning out. He hated her, was angry with her. That much she could tell without having spoken to him. Days before, everything had been different. She had been confident that he would leave Carly for her, had been convinced that her newfound pregnancy would be the answer to securing Hayden for herself.

But now, now she wasn't sure of anything. She couldn't be sure of anything. But more importantly, she silently had no idea what to do. Anxiously she nodded to herself; he just needed time. Time to think everything over. Then he would realize that he truly did belong with her rather than Carly and they could begin to build their life together.

He wasn't going to leave her. He would be leaving Carly, of that much she convinced herself.

Twenty-Five

For a man who had just accomplished scoring a game winning goal, Hayden certainly didn't feel the pride and excitement that should have come along with the glorious moment. It was moments like those that he had dreamed of having as a boy growing up, envisioning playing professionally. He had wanted those moments desperately, every hockey player did. But to finally accomplish something that victorious should have been a thoroughly glorious moment, but it failed to be such.

He had struggled to paint the smile across his face, to emit the joy that seemed to have overwhelmed his teammates, to express the excitement he knew he should be feeling. But the recent events of his life had shrouded any hope of enjoying such a glorious moment.

As he drove home, feeling the aches the game had brought him, he sighed, wishing he could simply drive, drive for hundreds of miles away from Carly, Lacey, his family and the world in general. Where no one would know him, and he could completely forget everything that had happened to him, the mistakes he now acknowledged he had made.

For a man used to always having the answer to every problem, always ready to find a solution to anything and everything, he was lost. Completely lost without the slightest clue, the longer he thought about it, he knew he should confess his affair to Carly, but there was no way that he could.

His affair, at this point, would ruin everything. He needed Carly, needed her in his life. One day, one day after their marriage was sound and secure again, he would tell her. He had to. He couldn't live with the guilt for the rest of his life. And slowly, they would work through that as well, but not now. They had enough to focus on, enough to work through as it was, to add the affair would only complicate things.

But then, there was Lacey, pregnant with his child. She wasn't exactly going to go away. She was after all Carly's best friend. Carly would eventually learn that Lacey was pregnant, and would instantly question as to who the father was. Carly knew that Lacey didn't have a boyfriend, as did the rest of the world that seemed to be interested in their personal lives.

Again as he reviewed their conversation he still couldn't come to terms with the fact that she had had enough nerve to ask him to leave Carly, and she hadn't exactly asked, mostly demanded. How could she ask him to leave his wife? She had known and knew just how much he loved her, how much he had wanted his marriage to return to how it had been before the miscarriage, that he had missed his wife through the past weeks. And that he had only sought her company as a vent, an excuse to escape the suffocating feeling of it all.

That's all she was to him. But how could he tell her that? It was one thing to simply end an affair, to say goodbye to a single individual person. But when that person was pregnant with your child, it simply wasn't that simple. That child was a piece, a part of him. Connected him to Lacey in a way that he had never imagined. That forever would be his child, and Lacey would forever be its mother.

It was easy to keep an affair from your spouse, but when there was a pregnancy, it complicated everything. But what wasn't complicated in his life any more. Angrily he tapped his fingers against the steering wheel. He would have to tell Carly. Would have to be honest with her about the entire affair, about the baby. Lacey wouldn't stay silent for long. Eventually she was going to demand an answer, a response of any kind. Something he simply didn't have.

He had no idea what he was going to tell Lacey. How did a man tell a woman pregnant with their child that they no longer wanted anything to do with them? How was a man supposed to be responsible in a situation like this? He had no idea how to help Lacey, how to help that baby. It deserved a father, but what kind of a father could he be, married to another woman, the woman that wasn't the mother to his child?

As he sat in his car, taking a few moments to himself before he walked into his home, he watched as Sal appeared in the window, his paws lifted to the window seat to peer out at the vehicle that had pulled into his driveway.

Despite the small smile that came to his face, he acknowledged just how horribly unfair the circumstances were for Carly. He would eventually confess his love and willingness to slowly work on their marriage, yet he would be holding back one important secret.

But again he reminded himself that telling Carly about the affair would only devastate her. Devastate her in a way that would devastate him. He had never dreamed of hurting the one person he loved, and to see her hurting, only hurt him more. And it wasn't just admitting to his affair, but it was also to a pregnancy. Carly wanted children more than anything. She was going to be more than jealous to learn that Lacey was not only pregnant but pregnant with his child.

To know that he would have to lie to Carly crushed him and applied a wave of guilt he had never known before. It had been easier to be cheating on her when he had convinced himself that she didn't care about him.

The problems began to mount with their endless questions with answers that evaded him. There was no possible way to fix this situation. But yet, he had to. He was tired of being plagued with constant voice mails and calls from Lacey asking if he was finally ready to talk. It had grown more and more difficult to avoid her, being the captain of the Jets who would be struggling their way through round two of the playoffs. Those reasons and more had finally brought him to the realization that he had to talk to Lacey. Had to tell her the truth, there was no way around it.

Twenty-Six

Lacey was slightly excited and relieved by the fact that Hayden had finally contacted her. She had spent at least a week and a half without sleep, struggling to focus at work, constantly wondering about her current circumstances. Eagerly she glanced at the clock. Fifteen more minutes until Hayden arrived to meet her. Fifteen more minutes till Hayden wrapped his strong arms around her, holding her close to tell her that he was hers, that he had left Carly, that now, they could begin to build their life together to raise their child.

Finally, when she felt as if she were about to burst with her impatience, the knock resounded on her hotel door. She kept herself from squealing as she rushed to open it, "Hayden!" she smiled broadly, confidently, as she held the door back. But her smile vanished instantly.

"Hey." He said lightly, a strange expression clouding his face. He seemed hesitant, no, not hesitant, sad, maybe more scared. She pushed the expression from her thoughts as she pushed ahead, "I'm so glad you're here!" Eagerly she wrapped her arms around him, taking in his smell of strong cologne.

"Um," he said uneasily, pulling her away from him gently, "I think you should sit down."

Slightly confused, she took her place on the edge of the bed. "Hayden, are you all right?"

"Would you just listen for a second?" he asked impatiently, his voice rising. When she nodded dumbly, he continued, "Lacey, I'm not leaving Carly, I'm not going to divorce her. She called me two nights ago to let me know that she is coming home for awhile, to attempt working things out." He exhaled a shaky breath, "I'm sorry, I truly am, about this baby, this affair, I know what I am about to say is going to hurt you, but you need to understand that I don't love you. I can't be with you anymore.

"But that baby is mine, I will own up to that, and I will take responsibility for it. I'll make sure that your financial means are provided for. I can at least do that much for you, I have to."

Her heart pounded against her chest, her thoughts swirling. What? Had he just said he wasn't leaving Carly? That he was providing financial means to care for the baby and herself? No, it wasn't possible. "No." she heard herself say. "You love me."

The frustration poured through, "No, Lacey, I don't. I love Carly, my wife. I want to stay with her."

The hurt that was causing the tears to stream down her cheeks quickly turned into anger. Pure loud anger, "How dare you!" she screamed viciously. "I am pregnant with your child! Your baby! You are supposed to love me! She doesn't love you!" she spat.

"She does." Hayden struggled to keep his voice calm and controlled, understanding that her reaction was to be expected.

"No, no, that's not why you're staying with her. She told you she's pregnant didn't she. You're leaving me and my baby because she's pregnant!"

The look that overcame his chiseled features was enough to cause her to stop ranting. She looked at him carefully, watching as clear understanding and then sudden disbelief clouded his eyes. "What?" he voiced quietly.

Complete horror filled her, "You didn't know?" she asked barely above a whisper. He shook his head lamely. What had she just done? Any hope of salvaging their relationship to make this work had just been shattered. Now that she had just told him that Carly was pregnant he was sure to go back to her.

"She's pregnant?" he whispered.

Unable to back track, take back what was said, she took a shaky breath of her own, "Yes, she's pregnant."

He looked completely shattered, "She's pregnant?"

How many times was she going to have to say it? "YES!" She screamed at him, suddenly completely disgusted with him. "Get out!" she stormed, "Get out!" she pushed him with as much force as she could muster.

Caught off guard he stumbled a bit to reclaim his balance, suddenly acknowledging that she was asking him to leave. With hatred pouring energy into force, she slammed the door shut. Weakly she crumpled against the door, pulling her knees against her chest. With heat she felt the tears finally break through, rushing as they slid onto the collar of her blouse. No, no it simply wasn't happening! He was supposed to love her!

As she remained there, crumpled on the floor, she shook with anger, the reality of her sudden situation settling in. She was alone, and pregnant. The embarrassment suddenly dawned on her. She had forced herself to believe that he loved her? That he had wanted to be with her? She had given everything to Hayden, and for what, to watch him go back to Carly as he abandoned her?

She stood, there had to be a way to make him hurt as much as she was. To make him pay for what he had done. It was then that the idea hit her. Anxiously she picked up her phone, digging through her purse to look for the tabloid number that had been willingly given to her months ago. Having had no plans to ever use the number she had thrown it into her purse until she could throw it away. But now, now she was thankful she had kept it.

Eagerly she tapped her foot with impatience while the number rang. Finally there was an answer, "Hello?" she sniffed to control her emotions, "I have a story that I think you will find interesting."

"Who's the celebrity?" the sneering voice asked.

"Well he's not a HollyWood celebrity, just a super star athlete."

"And?" the voice implored sarcastically.

"Hayden Alterson." Instant curiosity poured through. "And what do you have to share about him?" She took a moment to control her voice; she had to sound serious, "I was raped by Hayden Alterson."

Twenty-Seven

Having returned home to find Hayden gone, she had greeted Sal warmly. Oh, how good it was to be home! She had taken the time to unpack the small suitcase and had wandered through the house to become familiar with it again. After realizing around noon that she was hungry, she had headed to the kitchen, immediately surprised to find that the fridge was empty, save for a carton of milk. Hayden obviously hadn't been shopping for himself, and had more than likely been eating with Calvin and Mandy.

That simply wouldn't continue. She was home now, the rightful wife, who apparently wasn't being spared her duties. A grocery trip was in store for her. Sighing she reached for her car keys, headed to the car. Twenty minutes later she was making her way down the familiar grocery aisles, strangely aware that something was different.

Each aisle she travelled down people stopped to look at her, whispering to one another while a copy of a tabloid sat clutched in their hands. Not connecting the tabloid to the whispering, she pulled out her compact mirror, wondering if something was out of place. Finding nothing wrong with her makeup, and her clothes clean, she shrugged, pushing her cart forward.

By the time she reached the checkout, she was even more aware and troubled by the brief glances and occasionally pointing fingers. Deciding that she was in a hurry and wanting to be free from this strange experience, she rushed to place her items on the belt. After all of her groceries had been placed, she waited impatiently behind the woman ahead of her, silently wondering why the cashier couldn't move the line along any faster.

It was then that it caught her attention. The bold headline of a tabloid read, *"Alterson Capable of Rape?"* instantly intrigued she reached for the tabloid, pulling it from the rack. Upon further examination she read the sub line, *"Lacey Peterson in shambles after rape."* A sense of horror filled her as the words began to finally make sense to her. She felt her breathing shorten, immediate panic rising. There, on the front page, was a picture of herself, then Hayden and Lacey.

Immediate understanding took place. People were recognizing her as Hayden's wife, the wife of a man suddenly accused of raping her best friend! Without a second thought she abandoned her groceries, half running through the doors into the parking lot. Angrily she climbed behind the wheel of her car, speeding away to join the traffic. She had to find Hayden.

Hayden turned his head at the sound of his nickname, watching as Calvin approached him, a tabloid in hand. "What do you make of this?" Calvin stretched the tabloid to him; and with a furrowed brow, he took it, scanning the front page. It took him only a few seconds to read the headline then the sub lines, and see the picture of himself and Lacey. His heart rate immediately increased, the blood drained from his face and he felt his hands begin to shake. This couldn't be happening. She couldn't have, wouldn't have done something as extreme as this.

"How could they print a lie such as that!" Calvin looked at him with a confused expression, obvious disgust furrowing his brow.

Hayden couldn't bring himself to answer him. Instead he stood and walked out of the dressing room. He wasn't sure where he was going, but he had to go somewhere, had to find somewhere to be alone. The first place he spotted was Coach's office. He opened the door and slammed it behind himself, locking it, then pulling the blinds down. Dumbfounded he sat down in the office chair and folded the tabloid out across the desk.

"NHL Super Star Hayden Alterson Capable of Rape?" He read the headline aloud to himself now. *"Versus reporter Lacey Peterson admitted to sources yesterday evening that she was finally willing to step forward and shed light to a darker side of Alterson's personality. Peterson stated that Alterson had forced her into a room where he then raped her. Lacey said she failed to step forward sooner out of fear, fear of Altesron, and fear from her network franchise Versus.*

"Lacey said it was time that she brought healing and help to herself by sharing her story. She wanted to be a voice for all women who have been sexually assaulted and hopes her personal journey with this crisis brings closure and help to others."

He couldn't force himself to read the rest of the article, suddenly feeling nauseated. How could she? How could she tell such a blatant lie as that? It was an affair, an affair!

He lifted his head as he heard a knock on the door. "Hades, let me in."

Hayden stood to unlock the door, and took a step back as Cavin entered. "What am I going to do?" he ran a hand through his hair, "What am I supposed to do?"

Calvin studied his friend carefully, "It's not true….is it?"

Hayden felt the air leave his lungs, finally realizing that he was going to have to share everything. "No, well, yes, half of it anyways. It was an affair Cal, an *affair*, not rape. I told her that I was ending things. That I was going back to Carly. I made a mistake, a huge mistake Calvin."

Calvin sat quietly for a few moments, reading the article, "This is going to change things."

"I know that." Hayden threw his hands into the air. Everything was about to change, absolutely everything. He felt like vomiting, felt like digging a hole and burrowing himself in it. "The franchise is going to want to speak with you. Law enforcement will investigate this."

"I know." Was all Hayden could bring himself to say, "I know."

"You're going to have to tell the truth, in a press conference. You'll need an alibi, and a reputable lawyer." Calvin paused for a moment, "Hayden have you told Carly yet?"

Hayden took another shaky breath, "No."

"You should tell her Hayden before she reads it for herself somewhere."

Hayden struggled to nod, knowing his brother was right. "I know that too."

"You sure know a lot, but what are you going to do about it?"

Hayden sat back down again, "The hard thing....I have to tell Carly."

Twenty-Eight

The nausea increased as soon as Hayden saw Carly's vehicle parked in the driveway. As he opened the door he thought seriously about pulling back into traffic, driving back to the arena, hiding out there until he had put together more of a plan. He still didn't have any idea what he was going to say. How exactly did one tell his wife that he was involved in an affair, that his mistress was her best friend, and to add the cherry to the sundae, she was pregnant with his child.

He sighed hurriedly, cautiously turning the doorknob; but to his shock and surprise, the door swung back with force, Carly standing behind it, arms folded evenly across her chest. The slight sense of hope he had somewhat built up deflated the moment he saw her expression. How she had heard, how she had found out, he wasn't sure, but it was clear that she knew something was wrong.

"What is this!" He would have preferred her to scream at him, rather than the sadistic tone she spoke with. In all the time he had known her he had never seen her this angry or confused. The hurt was clearly expressed in her eyes.

He gulped, crumpling the tabloid in his hands, scrambling to find someway to explain himself. "I can explain," he said lamely, the words disappearing regardless of how many he had thought to use.

She nodded slowly, "I should hope so."

Taking a few seconds to pace their kitchen, he finally blurted, "I didn't rape her; it was an affair."

Carly closed her eyes, leaning against the fridge to steady herself. She had hoped, had hoped so desperately that she would not hear those words. Driving home she had rationalized a thousand different scenarios to explain the tabloid claim. Obviously something had happened that involved Hayden to put him in a tabloid spotlight.

But of all the scenarios, an affair had frightened her the most. There were many things she could forgive him for, but an affair was not one of them. She had watched how an affair had ruined her mother and had vowed the same would never happen to her. Yet, here she stood, a victim herself.

"Carly," Hayden struggled for words, "I didn't mean, I mean you have to believe me, you honestly think I'm capable of rape?"

She opened her eyes then, looking at him evenly, "That's what your worried about?" Among the hurt and confusion, anger suddenly overwhelmed her. "You're concerned that I might not believe you didn't rape her?" shaking her head she reached for the tabloid laying on the counter, the headline proclaiming Hayden's sins clearly visible.

"You have ruined me!" she spat angrily throwing the paper at him now, "You were supposed to love me, supposed to protect me, supposed to be there for me! This, this is how you accomplish those things?"

"I do love you." He floundered to explain himself.

"Love, Hayden, does not involve sleeping with another woman, your wife's best friend at that! You couldn't have sunk to any lower extremes!"

He shook his head now, "What, what was I supposed to do? You hated me, our marriage had fallen apart!" A new anger began to take hold of him, yes, he had involved himself in an affair, but he wasn't completely to blame was he? She had some ownership in this too!

Carly couldn't believe the words he had just spoken. He was actually blaming her for this? Blaming her for his affair, for his actions? His compromise? "Unbelievable." She spat. "You think you can turn around and blame me for this?"

"Not blame you, but you helped." Nervously he ran a hand through his hair, "I loved you, still love you, and you wouldn't let me help you, wouldn't let me share that hurt. You weren't the only one hurting Carly, that miscarriage affected more than just you!"

Stunned, she rested her arms on the counter top, but he continued before she had a chance to say anything, "I needed you, and you pushed me away! I was your husband, Carly; I am your best friend! We were supposed to share everything together. But it doesn't exactly surprise me, you would rather do everything yourself, you couldn't even tell me you were pregnant!"

The air left her lungs as she slowly understood what he had just said. There had been only one person she had confessed her secret to. Lacey was her best friend, she had trusted her above all others, but she had not only involved herself in an affair with her husband. She had told him about her pregnancy. Anger turned to rage as she glared at him, "She told you?"

"If she didn't who would have? Certainly not you!"

She nodded her head, "Your right Hayden. Lacey has all the answers doesn't she, in fact, if she was enough to help you through our troubled marriage, maybe you should go back to her!" she reached for the first thing she could grab and threw it at him with as much force as she could muster.

The pen bounced and clattered against the dishwasher. Hayden stooped down to slowly pick it up. He could understand her hatred, the hurt he had caused her. He knew he was to blame, but how could he explain his own frustrations and hurt? It didn't make him happy or proud to see and know that he had caused that hurt.

Exhausted trying to figure out what to say, he approached her slowly, "Carly," he struggled to control his voice, the unashamed tears threatening to spill, "I love you. I haven't done right by you, but please, you were willing to come back, you were willing to at least attempt at working out our marriage. It's just not us to think about any more, we have a baby Carly, a child that is going to need us. We have to try to make this work."

She resisted his effort to embrace her, pulling away sharply. Angrily she shook her head, completely disregarding his plea, "No Hayden. No, it will never work. I made an exception once, but you had an affair. Lacey solved your problems for you, but yet, look at you now." Eagerly, she picked up the tabloid, pressing it against his chest with force, "You created this mess, and you're about to suffer the consequences, without help from me. If you truly had loved me, you wouldn't have gone to her!"

Biting her lip, she closer her eyes, attempting to gather some bravery to say the words she hadn't wanted to. "I want a divorce Hayden. This marriage is over." Anxiously, she reached for her keys, heading towards the door.

Hayden crumpled onto a barstool, resting his head in his hands, "Carly, please, please don't say that! I never expected this, I never expected her to do this!"

The words were enough to cause her to stop in her tracks. Her anger multiplied as she whirled to face him from the entryway, "What did you think Hayden, that you could have an affair and keep it from me? That all of this would just stay quiet?" she looked at him, took in how pathetic he looked clinging to the barstool. As she stood there, it suddenly dawned on her another possible meaning behind his words, "Hayden, she asked you to leave me didn't she."

How was it possible for her to know that? Hayden scrambled for an answer, "I told her that things had to end, that I wanted to work things out with you. That I would help her financially with the baby." He realized he had gone too far as soon as he said the words.

"Baby?" Carly's eyes grew round, "She's pregnant, Hayden?" there were no words to describe the hate beaming from her eyes.

"Yes." As he sat there looking at her, he floundered suddenly realizing his own anger, "I found out about her pregnancy before ours."

Taken aback Carly looked away, the rage mounting all the more. Lacey had been her best friend! She had confided in her!

Carly allowed a moment of silence to settle between them, "I can't believe this, I can't believe you!" she spat angrily. There was no need for any of this. Not to mention that everyone in the world was suddenly aware of their current situation. She was married to a super star athlete who had failed to be faithful to her, cheating on her with not some random but her claimed best friend! Suddenly unable to take any more and filled with disgust, she continued her walk to the door. Before turning the go she said quietly, "I thought we could make this work Hayden. I wanted you to find out about this baby differently, but obviously that wasn't meant to happen."

"Where are you going?" he stood up behind her, suddenly realizing she was standing in front of the door.

"Away Hayden. Away from you!" she spat angrily. "I can't stay here. I can't keep putting myself through this hurt Hayden. Before, the hurt was forgiveable, but this, Hayden, this I don't know." She shook her head angrily, tears spilling against her cheeks, "I was going to tell you that I wasn't going to file for divorce, but now, now, you've only helped me to decide. This marriage is done Hayden. It's over."

The words left a sorrow unlike any he had felt before, a dull, forceful, pounding hurt. "Carly, please." He pleaded again, his voice breaking now.

She stood there, for a few moments, as if carefully reconsidering. And for a brief moment he felt hope. "No, Hayden. It's over. My lawyer will be in contact with you." Hayden remained on the barstool, the horrid realization sinking in.

This time Carly had left for good. She had asked for a divorce, had said there was no hope to repair their marriage. The sorrow was unbearable as he allowed himself to acknowledge that this time, there was no hope of Carly coming back.

Dear Reader,

I wanted to take a moment to share a few words with you personally. I thank you for reading this story that God has given me to share with you, and hope you enjoyed it just as much as I did writing it. However, I can understand if you have been confused by the rather abrupt ending of this story, I cannot apologize for that, for that is where God wanted it to end for the time being. But do not worry, in his timing, there will be more to come!

I hope that through this story you were able to see Hayden's compromise and the consequences that will follow. Just as Hayden, I think we all find ourselves in a circumstance where we have made a mistake, or have compromised in our faith.

I know I personally have, we are all human, and we are not perfect.

The most important thing to remember however, is that in the midst of consequence, and hurt that may have followed because of a mistake we have made, we still need God, and He still loves us.

Regardless of what you have done, God loves you. Always has, and always will. He has made the ultimate sacrifice, by accepting death by a cross that should have been rightfully ours. Because He loves us this much, he is able to look past whatever you have done, whatever mistake we have made, and wrap us in His arms and take away our hurt and our shame.

I cannot personally relate to you, just how wonderful it is to know that there is a God who loves us this much, and what a freedom it is to be able to trust in Him. God has never done anything to hurt me, and never will, working all things for my better, even through my mistakes.

My prayer for you as you journey through life, and your faith, is that you will seek Him, and lean on him. Leaning on those everlasting arms of love and reassurance. He has never let you go, and never will.

If you do not have a personal relationship with Him, he is eagerly awaiting for you to accept him, and it could not have been made more simple. Admit to God you are a sinner, believe that Jesus is God's son, and confess your sins, ask for his forgiveness. There is no judgment there, only freedom His love alone can bring.

I look forward to sharing the next story with you! Until next time,

Holly Hands